THE SHIITAKE ADVENTURE COMPANY

BY
RICK BUTTS

Coyote Creek Press

The Safari Adventure Company

Copyright© 1997
Rick Butts
All rights reserved

First Printing August 1996
Second Printing January 1997

ISBN 09652991-4-7

Coyote Creek Press, Houston
E-mail: rick@butts.com
http://www.butts.com
1-800-442-6214

No part of this book may be reproduced or transmitted in any form including: electronic, mechanical, photocopying, recording, or information storage and retrieval systems; without prior written permission from the author.

ACKNOWLEDGMENTS

One of the greatest mistakes anyone can make is to labor under the illusion that he does anything significant alone. Heartfelt thanks to the following folks who made this second edition of the Safari possible!

TO:

John Wilson for believing in me when no one else did.

Joe Vitale, the incredible wizard or words and the king of copywriters!

Brocky and Nancy Brown, whose Brockton Publishing Co. sure can make books.

Toni Griffin, the small but loud voice who insisted I write and that this story must be told.

Jim Rohn, Brian Tracy, and Denis Waitley, who woke me up and set me on the journey.

John MacArthur Jr. whose teaching brought me the real truth.

My awesome mother, Nancy, who gave me the gift of believing in myself.

To my Father, Ron who taught me to balance strength and kindness.

Most of all to my loving wife and life partner Glenna and daughter Rachael, my incredible barrel racing, rodeo queens. Happy forever under the nickel moon!

Table of Contents

The Safari Adventure Company	9
The Office	29
The Park	43
Africa	53
Heros and Legends	66
The Lake of Stars	83
The First Treasure	91
Wilderness	115
The Second Treasure	131
Ancient Adventurers	147
African Storm	159
Hopelessly Lost	163
The Third Treasure	179
Dangerous Rescue	197
Over and Out	213

Introduction to the Three Treasures

The Royal Safari Adventure Company
1895 London, England

We, the members in good stead with the Royal Safari Adventure Company, do herewith set forth our great hope that you, the reader, will avail yourself of the wisdom contained on these pages. The principles here are time-tested and strong. You need know from the beginning that you will always be as unhappy as you are this otherwise fine day, unless you come to realize that happiness does not lie on the outerside of your life.

If you seek fulfillment in the 'things' of this reality, you are doomed to be ruled by circumstance, unforeseeable luck, and the whims of others who care not a whit for you or your lot. These will be your masters as you struggle to fill the void in your life with the stuff of materialism. For you see, dear voyager, you will never be truly happy until you gain the understanding that joy is to be found inside of you. There are certain joys, we call them treasures, that you may possess despite the winds of change that blow on us all. The Three Treasures herein will serve you well if you recall to measure and add to them every day. Neglect to care for them often, and you will go there one day to find them gone, sifted away a little at a time like flour through a hole in the bottom of a miller's sack.

Gather these treasures, for they are there for everyone. Seek them and your life will be richer than any King who lies awake at night, sleepless despite his rooms filled with gold. Protect them, never let anyone trick you into trading them for the passing pleasures of this world, and they will comfort you in your golden years and put you at peace about the life beyond.

THE SAFARI ADVENTURE COMPANY

"I must be nuts to even consider this! She would kill me if she knew I was here!" Jim looked across the street at the curious shop.

"I should just leave. I've got to finish this awful report." His finger tapped the manila folder sticking out of the khaki canvas bag he used for a briefcase. Just thinking about the problem at work made his stomach hurt again.

He sat in the parking lot across the street in his dark green Ford Explorer and pulled the yellow flyer out of his pocket one more time.

THE SAFARI ADVENTURE COMPANY
"The Greatest Adventure is the Rest of Your Life!"

Just This Once, You Owe It To Yourself To See How You Measure Up Against A Real Challenge!

Choose From Many Different Lands, Climates, And Situations. This Is No Disneyland, *This Is An Odyssey!*

For More Information, call 409-826-2371

Jim had always played it safe. Never in his life had he allowed himself to be put in a position where he might lose. Carefully playing the odds, he had constructed a false world of security. Like most of the people he knew, the momentum of mediocrity had captured him. Somehow, though, he was beginning to sense the pain of realizing it.

Jim remembered a guy at work handing him the ad about a month ago. It had seemed hokey and funny at the time. He had intended to show it to Tracey, his wife, but it had gotten stuck in one of the drawers at the office and forgotten. That was until yesterday, when he had come across it as he searched the files for information on the terrible problem at the plant.

His eyes were drawn back again to the quaint little shop. On one side was a Chinese restaurant. On the other was a savings and loan. A small free-standing, red brick building housed the Safari Adventure Company, American Headquarters. The antique brass and green sign looked like something from London, circa 1800. A large glass window filled to clutter with all sorts of curious telescopes, helmets, a ship's wheel, and countless other interesting objects, beckoned a closer look.

Feeling self conscious and more than a little bit silly, Jim unfolded himself from the Explorer. He was tall, but the sales woman assured him at the dealership that taller people had been very happy with the "sport utility vehicle," as she called it. It was a little tight behind the wheel but he wanted the Explorer so much he bought it anyway. He just liked the way it made him feel.

He examined himself in the side mirror and pushed a stray black lock, flecked with silver, back into place. "Not bad for 41!" he said to himself, his blue eyes flashing their boyish smile. Some of his friends were already bald. His forehead was getting a little larger but he still had a respectable crop if you moved it around a little.

He grabbed his soft wool jacket from the back seat and slipped it on. Tracey called it the "business casual look." It was difficult for him to quit wearing the pinstripes at first, but she started him just on Fridays for a while. Now he really preferred the khaki slacks and denim shirt he wore today. He straightened his brightly colored silk tie, hiked his pants up over his American paunch, and turned to cross the street.

The heavy oak and glass door swung in easily to Jim's push, jingling the leather strapped sleigh bells used by busy shopkeepers. There was a lot to see and since no one was there at the moment, Jim tried to take it all in. The place looked like a cross between a trophy den in an explorer's home and a souvenir stand at a carnival. There were posters from far away places, gifts, no doubt, from the thankful travel agencies they used for their tours. There were dozens of trophy animal heads and fresh and saltwater fish staring intently from every wall. Some of them were adorned with hats, sunglasses and other trinkets, giving even the ferocious tiger a strangely funny and harmless appearance. Instead of displaying a fierce snarl, the tiger seemed to smile. Jim smiled back.

Voices were talking excitedly in the rear of the office. One had some kind of accent, but Jim could not identify it. Perhaps, it was British. Within a minute of waiting, no one had come out to greet him, and Jim began to get cold feet.

The lady who had answered the telephone when he had called for information earlier had been a little evasive and would not give out many details. She insisted that Jim could not simply choose to sign up but, rather, would have to come in and apply. She told him he would have to pass a test. Not everyone could qualify. The challenge was very rigorous.

This had to be a big sales gimmick. You know, the kind where they entice you to just come by and see what free gift you are eligible for, and then they give you the old, hard sell. The old take-away close! he thought. They make you think you can't have what they offer, which only makes you want it more, and at their high price! Well, they were dealing with old Shopper-Jim now, and he wasn't about to fall for any tricks. They're probably back there hammering on some poor soul right now.

Just then, his problems at home and work began silently poking their fingers in his chest. He tightened his jaw. Oh, this is stupid! I can't be running off to some crazy dude ranch, he thought, to himself. The smell of the Chinese food teased him to consider an early dinner.

Just as Jim reached for the door to leave, a sound came roaring down the hall and into the waiting room. It was laughter. Not just an ordinary laugh either. This was one of those deep, rich, robust belly laughs that starts with an unexpected burst and turns into a wheezing, gasping attempt to speak that is denied words by the force of whatever hilarious affliction began it all. You can't help but laugh when you hear one of those plastic, battery-operated "giggle boxes" they sell in novelty shops, and you couldn't help but want to laugh at this raucous "haw-haw-haw" belting down the hall. Jim smiled, in spite of himself, and tried hard not to chuckle.

When was the last time he had laughed like that? The happy sound, so robust and carefree, contrasted with the knot of tension that seemed to live in his chest full-time. Jim sat down on the couch and decided to see this thing at least to the next step. Something was telling him to stay.

The coffee table in front of him looked to be made from an old ship's door. He ran his fingers over the rusty hinges and weathered wood, now varnished and smooth and picked up a travel magazine. As he thumbed through, he started reading an article about kayaking down a river in Asia. The water looked so blue and cold next to the bright orange kayaks and yellow outfits of the people in the pictures. It sure looked like fun, but dangerous, too.

The crystal clear photographs and descriptions pulled him in. He was right there, shooting the rapids. The roaring of the river filled his ears, when, suddenly, the voices in the back room were joined by the movement of chairs. Footsteps down the hall indicated they were coming toward the front. Jim pretended to read the magazine.

"Hullo there, sir!" called out a large man, sticking out a bear paw sized hand toward Jim. "Didn't hear you come in, I guess. Benjamin at your service, sir! Welcome to the Safari Adventure Company! And who might you be?"

He was a giant! His khaki pants and vest over a plaid flannel shirt certainly looked the part. The English accent and the overwhelming appearance of the man took Jim by surprise. His sandy hair and full beard reminded Jim of a backwoods trapper, and the smiling eyes pulled you in like a target. Jim stood right up and shook hands. He used a tighter grip than normal as he gazed upward into the bearded face. Jim was just over 6' tall and not used to looking up at many people. He sensed how funny it felt, like he was a kid.

Jim introduced himself and stammered something about seeing the ad and calling.

"Smashin'! You'll do just great!" complimented Benjamin, which served to both encourage and make Jim suspicious of the "qualification" part.

"This here is Todd. He went on his first safari

with us about two years ago. Tell 'em, Todd. Is it worth the time?"

At this point, the young man who had come down the hall with Benjamin, turned rather shyly toward Jim and smiled. Todd was about Jim's age and wore a dark navy suit and tie. There was a distinct sparkle in his eyes as he said simply, "Whatever you do, don't miss the opportunity to go. It'll change your life forever!"

With that, Todd turned back to Benjamin. They shook hands enthusiastically and said good-bye.

As Jim was watching Todd leave, Benjamin put his arm on Jim's shoulders and said, "Come on now, mate. I'll bet you've got a million questions. First of all, I'm Australian." He pointed him down the hall to his office.

The office was a bit messy, but comfortable. There were pictures everywhere. Jim noticed a candle burning on the back credenza and sniffed the pleasant smell of sandalwood.

"I just like the way it smells." Benjamin said. "I read the other day that one of the trends in our society is that people are treatin' themselves to small indulgences. You know, bub, flavored coffees and the like."

"How did you get into this business, Benjamin?" asked Jim, trying to think of something bright to say as the two men sat down at the desk.

"I went on a safari, of course. Everyone who works for the company started out as a customer. Once you've been on one yourself, it will be easier to see why that happens." Benjamin said pretending to straighten his papers.

"Have you guys been in business very long? I've never heard of you?" asked Jim.

"Oh, my word, mate, yes! The Company has been around for quite a long time. It was started in London in 1856 by a group of people who felt that the average bloke never got the chance to push themselves to their limits. Most people go through life pickin' the low hangin' fruit. You know, they get an education or some kind of trainin', then they plod right ahead into the job they trained for—victims of circumstance. I have met very few teenagers that had any serious idea at all what they wanted to do for the rest of their lives. From time to time they get restless and go crazy, some make changes, but most live a bit of a sad, bittersweet life wonderin' if there ain't more."

If there was one phrase that described how Jim was feeling, it was: "Isn't there more?" He even caught himself the other day singing the old Peggy Lee song, "Is That All There Is?" and he was not smiling.

"I don't mean to imply that a simple hometown life is wrong. I live that life myself now," Benjamin patted his belly. "What I mean is that there is somethin' deep down inside a heart that longs to be right smack-dab in the middle of a real adventure! There is a longin' for somethin' that can't be found in the ordinary go of things. Explorin' new places, seein' sights for the very first time, facin' real danger, and helpin' to be part of somethin' bigger than just a paycheck. Sometimes as a part of a team and sometimes just climbin' that last few hundred feet to the top of a mountain all alone.

It was true in 1856, and it is even truer today. A psychology magazine article last month confirmed what I've known all along. They said that 85% were unhappy or unfulfilled with their jobs and 50% would rather be married to someone else. Just look at the movies they watch and the games they play. Sex and violence, virtual reality battles, and they go out and buy a 4-wheel drive jeep when the roughest thing they face is an occasional pothole!"

Jim's mind flashed. He thought about his 4-wheel drive Explorer in the parking lot. He thought about the virtual reality game he had bought for his son and the cable television program he had recently seen that teased about virtual reality sex. He thought about how bored he often was with his job in the downsizing company. Though things were way too hairy at work now, once this blew over, the dull repetition of sameness and politics would resume again.

Benjamin's words were more than statistics to Jim. He had let the game of being married to someone else creep into his conscious mind with cautious enthusiasm more and more lately. It made him feel guilty, but he felt justified because he was sure Tracey felt the same way. There were no money, alcohol, or drug problems.

Their whole relationship was more like being roommates, except they had the kids.

"I could go on for days, you know, but I can see your time is valuable. What's your story, Jim?" asked Benjamin, "Exactly why are you here today?"

Jim snapped back and stammered, "Well, I got this flyer, and uh, I was wondering, you know, if this thing was for real and..."

"Lots of people see these flyers. Some call, but only a few actually come to see us."

The friendly Australian leaned forward, lowered his voice, and smiled as he looked Jim straight in the eye.

"There is another reason why you're here," said Benjamin softly. "What's really goin' on? Is somethin' troublin' you?"

This huge bear of a man was somehow very easy to trust. Ordinarily Jim kept things to himself. He never opened up to anyone and certainly not to a total stranger. The situation he was facing was unbearably difficult. He really wanted to get some input on it. At the sincere invitation, the words came tumbling out.

"All my life I have worked for this company," he began defiantly. "I have saluted the powerful, dressed in the uniform of everyone's expectations and taken my electronically transferred bacon home every week."

Benjamin grinned broadly and snorted a laugh at Jim's clever phraseology. Jim plowed ahead. He had kept this inside and told no one. Now he was on a roll.

"Whenever they needed something done, I made sure my name was called." He continued. "I was a good soldier. I always believed the company would be there for me, too. Now, I'm not so sure."

"What do you mean?"

"Two days ago one of the people on my team called me in to her office and shut the door. She was really upset. She showed me information that seemed to indicate my boss had pulled a real fast one with some safety equipment. I have a report for his boss due tomorrow afternoon. The figures don't add up. If I let this go and cover it up, I could get in big trouble."

Benjamin leaned forward across the desk and asked, "Did you check her story?"

"Yes, I did some research on the files for our division. It took some digging, but sure enough, my boss's fingerprints are there," said Jim sadly. "I believe he was trying to keep the project under budget to win a promotion."

"So what are you goin' to do?" Benjamin asked.

The question irritated Jim. He did not want to answer it now. In fact he had been putting off answering it all week.

"I don't know what to do." He took a deep breath and looked down at his hands. They didn't seem to be his hands. In fact they looked older somehow, more like his father's hands.

After a moment of intentional silence, Benjamin said, "Winston Churchill once said, The truth is incontrovertible. Malice may attack it, and ignorance may deride it, but in the end, there it is.'"

Jim thought about the words for a moment, nodding his head, then launched his rehearsed defense.

"If I stand up for this truth, my boss might get fired and nobody else will ever trust me again. In the politics of my company, if I get the reputation of a snitch, it could wreck my career." Jim began to argue with himself. Benjamin sat quietly and listened.

"But remaining silent would be wrong," said Jim. "My wife says I need to just go along with the boss and forget my so called moral dilemma', but it's really bothering me."

Jim felt as though he were somewhere else in the room, watching himself tell this stranger the most intimate corporate secrets. He was at once embarrassed at his own weakness and relieved to hear it out loud. It felt good to talk with Benjamin. It was the first time he had told another soul about his feelings, and it was cleansing.

Benjamin listened patiently as Jim continued to whine and flounder with his predicament. When he noticed the safari director studying him carefully, he paused, embarrassed. Benjamin allowed the silence to tell him Jim was finished. Then he looked Jim straight in the eye and said, "That is certainly a difficult challenge. What do you intend to do about it?

Jim was taken aback at the direct way Benjamin made it clear that he would have to come to his own conclusion and actions. Jim squirmed in his chair a bit and changed the subject by asking about the safari.

Benjamin explained it to him in detail. First, there would be a physical examination. The trips were indeed challenging and might include mountain climbing, rafting, hiking. Shooting safari's had been outlawed a long time ago. There would be no big game hunting. The idea of needless slaughtering was never a part of the original founders' plan.

Benjamin promised some out-of-this-world dining! The food would include local exotic fare. As Benjamin described delicious feasts and particularly one salted venison dish he loved, topped with a sweet date pudding, Jim realized he was salivating. He swallowed and touched the tip of his tongue to his lips slightly, and thought about the Chinese restaurant again.

The sightseeing was designed to access some of the remotest and most beautiful places on earth. Benjamin handed Jim a full brochure that made his mouth drop open in wonder. A big grin invaded his face and his eyes sparkled as he transported himself right there into the picture.

There would be a training seminar and preparation at their facilities before departing by plane to Africa. Once there, they would undertake the safari which would include jeep travel to some of the most fascinating game preserves in the world. They would definitely encounter big game! The time in Africa would conclude with a banquet with the other safari adventurers before returning to their homes around the world. The entire program would take about 17 days.

It sounded very interesting. There was one big question left to ask. "Benjamin, how much does this whole thing cost?" Jim braced, ready to flinch at the number.

Benjamin grinned from across the desk as though this was his favorite part of the sales pitch. "It doesn't cost a dime," he said.

"What?" Jim exclaimed incredulously. Leaning forward and turning his head slightly as if he could possibly have had trouble hearing the high-volume Benjamin, he asked, "What did you say?"

"That's right. It's absolutely free! Now, of course, you have to buy your own clothes and incidentals, but the entire trainin', food, travel, really everythin' you'll need, is provided by the proceeds of a charitable annuity that was established around 1895. It was originally funded by the founders, and has grown by contributions from graduates of the Safari Adventure Company. In fact, in special cases we even provide scholarships for some people who cannot afford to take off from their work. We pay them a salary to go on the safari, so their family can still tend the home fires."

Jim was stunned. What was the catch? There had to be some kind of a "sign-away-your-first-born" clause. But, no matter how many questions Jim asked, Benjamin made it clear there was no obligation beyond the general release of liability. Any business that wanted to stay in business would ask for that in today's lawsuit-happy society.

"Here, take the application and agreement to your lawyer, if you like." Benjamin handed him two simple sheets of paper.

"Jim, I can see that you're a little confused. So was I. You're thinkin' maybe this company, or whatever it is, may have the dough for this nonsense and can afford to be loose with it. More importantly, you are wonderin' why on earth would they offer this to the public and especially to you? Perhaps this will help."

"Everyone has a hole inside them. Kind of like a void that ain't filled by anythin' money can buy, or any possession anyone can own. In fact, it can only be filled by unconditionally givin' to another human bein' somethin' that he needs to receive. The people who started the Safari Adventure Company, over a hundred years ago, knew this. They, and others that have followed, want to share the experience with others that come into our path. The person who handed you the flyer actually invited you.

Jim thought about the guy at work who handed him the flyer. He was very pleasant and well liked. He did not seem at all like someone who would walk on the wild side with something so far out as this. He flashed a mental picture of his co-worker hiking the rainforest in a suit.

"About the time a person reaches their fortieth birthday, they start to get real restless like." Benjamin said. "The natural rhythm of life causes them to take a long look at everythin'. They look at the past and the road they are on and ask themselves if they should continue, or make a change. What happens at that crossroads is absolutely critical!

The brief time you take to step back and carefully make these choices could be all the difference in the rest of your life. The safari gives you the perfect time and environment to do that. If I could help you to see from this office what you will know quite clearly by the end of the safari, you would beg me to let you come. Todd said it best earlier. Don't miss this opportunity. It really will change your life forever'."

There was a lot to think about. An offer you can't refuse, thought Jim. Smiling wistfully, he began to feel himself getting excited about the possibility of really going.

Some day.

"Take your time. Think it over." Benjamin said, smiling. "Call me whenever you like," he said handing Jim a beautiful business card in the shape of a treasure map. It was made of a rough parchment type paper and felt good just to hold.

One of those small indulgences, thought Jim as he placed it in his shirt pocket.

As they walked to the door, Benjamin pointed out some of the pictures on the wall and brief stories that smacked of fun and excitement.

"We go to a lot of places all over the world. The next safari is actually scheduled to be a sort of reunion.

The Safari Adventure Company

We are goin' to Africa!" he said again with a twinkle in his eyes. "If you go you will get to meet some of the oldest members of the Safari Adventure Company. There will be people who actually knew the foundin' members!" said Benjamin proudly. "There will be a banquet at the lodge in Africa before we set out into the bush. You will hear stories there beyond anythin' virtual reality ever hinted at!"

Finally, Jim thanked Benjamin. The young lady who had answered the phone when he had first called was back at the front desk eating a sandwich she had been out getting when he had arrived. Benjamin introduced Jim to her.

"Yes, I talked to you on the phone!" she said excitedly. "Glad you could make it in. You are going to Africa aren't you?"

She was a pretty girl in her early 20's with long brown hair and hazel eyes. Jim noticed she wore a T-shirt with the Safari Adventure Company Logo. He thought to himself it was the coolest T-shirt he had ever seen. The jungle scene with some type of ruins in the center and animals all around was capped with the gold letters of the company at the top. Across the bottom were the words, "THE GREATEST ADVENTURE IS THE REST OF YOUR LIFE!"

"I've got some things to check on and I, uh, well, I..." his voice trailed off.

"Sure you will, Jim!" she said nodding her assurance.

"OOPS! I almost forgot!" said Benjamin reaching

into the counter. "Here, this is for you. Sort of a gift for stoppin' by. I think you will enjoy it."

He handed him a small pocket-sized book with a fancy burgundy leather cover. Jim turned it over and looked at the front. The title was stamped in gold foil letters and said simply, "The Three Treasures", London, England 1895. Jim muttered about not being much of a reader, then thanked them both for everything. He carefully pulled the oak and glass door closed behind him, trying not to jangle the bells and left.

In a quiet, purposeful way, he guided his "jungle jeep" down the long way home through the country to think about everything Benjamin had offered. The sun was setting behind him. The world was turning pink, orange and fiery red in his rear view mirror. Only darkness seemed to lay ahead. His favorite jazz station rolled out a slow mellow blues number but Jim was oceans away. He was trekking across a golden savannah wearing a bush jacket, boots, and a wide brimmed canvas hat. He was parting large green leaves and peering into a clearing at some ancient ruins, searching for treasure.

A horn honked rudely as a kid in a sports car woke him to see he was drifting into the other lane. Jim pulled the wheel sharply to the right as the red convertible shot past him. An angry teenaged boy glared disapprovingly out of a blasting stereo sound. Jim settled down and began to think about what lay ahead.

Benjamin was right. He hadn't realized it, but he had been putting everything in his life on the table for examination the last few months. As the soft and steady music counted out the miles, he took another look at his world.

His loveless marriage... his painful work... his unfulfilled life... the hopeful safari...

It was Tuesday. By Friday it was all going to come down at work, big time! He would be forced to make a decision. He thought ofChurchill's words about truth. In the end, there it was.

THE OFFICE

"Hello, Jim. Mr. Jackson is expecting you. I was just taking him this file. I'll let him know you're here. You may have a seat, if you like," said Jackson's personal assistant.

He glanced through the door into the luxurious expanse of his boss's corner office.

"Jim!" called Jackson. "Come on in!"

The place was awesome; a regular trophy room. The elegant paneling tastefully presented with autographed photos of celebrities, company big shots, and wild game trophies, all brass name-plated, of course. It was an impressive fortress. The massive antique desk was the focal point. A serious piece of real estate, it rose in the lush carpet like a great temple to business success. Jackson stood quickly from behind it and moved around to shake Jim's hand. A stranger would have thought they were old friends.

"Thanks for coming on such short notice, Jim." Jackson smiled broadly. "Do you need some coffee or anything?"

Jackson's silver hair was cut a little long for the style of the day. His expensive dark blue suit was immaculate, like the office. No doubt about it, the boss had a taste for the finer things in life, and a way of getting them.

"No, I just had some, thanks," replied Jim as he settled into the leather guest chair, notebook on his lap.

He always felt like a visitor around Jackson. Some people had "relationships" with their boss. Jackson was careful to keep everyone at a safe distance. The secretary closed the heavy walnut door gently on the way out. Jackson sat on the corner of his desk and looked down at Jim. He seemed to study Jim for a moment, as if by looking at his eyes he could learn something more about what was inside. Jim swallowed dryly and waited, wondering how this would play. Finally Jackson spoke.

"Jimmy," (He had never called him Jimmy!) "I really need your help. There has been a bit of a hitch in the turbine project and I'm afraid it is going to cost the plant some money. Now the bottom line is this. I need you to sign some authorization forms here that show that I was not responsible for the mistakes. We are going to put it back down the line."

It was about to hit the fan and Jim wanted to duck. There was nowhere to hide

"Now I know that this is very irregular, but the safety nuts are already pestering us. If they can put an executive in the frying pan, they will, and make us all look like a bunch of jerks. This could cost the stockholders and basically make life tough for everyone in the plant and their families. We just don't need a

The Office

bunch of bad publicity right now if we can avoid it."

Well, there it was, thought Jim. It didn't take Jackson long to get to the bottom line. Jim sat smiling up at his so-called "superior." He always felt small around Jackson. A sensation, no doubt, Jackson intentionally created in all the people who reported to him.

"Gee, boss," he said with limp enthusiasm, "you know I have always been on your team."

He hated himself for the gutless words. He hated the sound of his voice. Couldn't he even talk to Jackson about what was going on?

As Jackson went on about the "little people", the workers, and how they depended on the management to look after them and their kids, Jim thought about his next move. Jackson knows I'm a team player. Heck, I've gone to the carpet for him before in the gray areas. He was so well connected in the company you just couldn't lose by being on his team! Jackson knew Jim was a loyal soldier, so why was he selling this so hard?

Though he did not like the taste of it, Jim resigned himself to roll over and follow the money and power. Just give me the papers and some "atta-boys" and say you will invite me to dinner soon. I can tuck those business IOU's in my career briefcase and let's get on with the favors! The favors Jim knew would follow.

"So I know I can count on you, Jimmy. You're a sharp guy and I promise I won't forget who was on my team when the game was on the line," continued Jackson. "This next project could be the feather in your cap. I was planning on putting you in charge, up front, where Flint could see your style!"

The moment of truth. Jim had never batted an eye lash before. He had always trusted his boss. He was trained that way. Like a dolphin at the Sea Park he was rewarded to respond. Just make the right hand sign and Jim would jump, spin, and resurface with a smile to claim the prize to the applause of the crowd. It always worked before. By golly, it was working again!

"You can count on me, sir." Jim smiled the company smile. "You know that. Where are these forms? I'll sign them now and get out of your hair."

"The papers will be ready Friday. Be here a little bit early so we can get them all in order for Mr. Flint," said Jackson, smiling again. "He will be in that afternoon."

"I thought he would be here today," questioned Jim.

"He was held up, so we got a little bit of breathing room. You have a great day and I will see you in the morning. And don't worry about Skinflint, I will handle him myself this time and take a little heat off you."

Everyone always referred to Jackson's boss as "Skinflint" for his ruthless money-saving programs. Jim had never heard Jackson refer to him by the nickname, his eyes showed his surprise.

"Yeah, Jimmy, we used to call him that back when he and I started working here together 25 years ago down in the maintenance crew sweeping floors. He was a jerk then, too!"

The Office

They both laughed together as Jackson put his arm around Jim and smiled. Jim instantly felt as if something foul and sick had fallen on him. He steered Jim toward his office door. Helpless, he went along.

"Thanks again, and see you in the morning," said Jackson. "You are a bright penny, Jimmy-boy. You're really going to go far!"

Jim punched the elevator button. He was heading down alright. He turned to see Jackson waving good-bye to him like a parent sending his small son to camp, as the doors drew closed. This was too much. Jackson was selling way too hard for Jim's cooperation on what seemed like a shady deal, no doubt, but not that big. What was Jackson was not telling?

Two hours later the lunchroom was already crowded by the time Jim arrived. He had almost overlooked the appointment until his secretary had reminded him. He had been so turned upside down by the meeting with Jackson that he had forgotten about "John from Sector 6". What ever it was this guy wanted, Jim thought, he would get it over with fast and get out. He was in no mood for favors.

"Over here, sir!" called out a worker in dirty overalls.

"What now?" Jim grumbled, realizing he'd been tricked. "Some low-life wrench-turner trying to brown-nose an executive. Well, I don't have time for this."

Jim pretended he hadn't seen the worker and

turned to leave, but the man moved quickly to his side and took Jim's arm.

"I'm your lunch meeting," the worker announced seriously.

Jim turned toward him, irritation clearly showing on his face. Glancing down at the man he could see the name badge. "John — Sector 6", it said simply.

Oh, my lucky day, he thought to himself. This will be a memorable event. How did this guy ever get a lunch with me?

"I am sorry to disturb you, sir, but it is very important that you talk with me. You need to hear what I have to say," apologized the worker.

John was in his late forties, and very fit. He was rather short and barrel chested with large Popeye-sized arms that denoted great strength and frequent use. His swept back black hair was neatly cropped. Dark eyes looked up at Jim and told him at once that he was very serious.

They moved silently through the cafeteria line. Jim loaded up. John chose a small sandwich.

As they sat down, Jim dove into his food then glanced up to find John bowing his head, folding his hands together, and closing his eyes over his sandwich.

Was this guy praying? Jim looked back down at his plate, flushed with embarrassment. Everyone in the lunchroom must be looking at them. What would they think? Thankfully, it didn't last long. Jim took another bite and scanned the tables sheepishly to see who was

The Office

in the cafeteria that might joke with him about it later. He then waited in obvious irritation for John to begin.

"I work in the drilling division," John announced quickly.

"What does that have to do with me?" Jim asked impatiently. "You are in 6 and I am in 23."

John began again deliberately. "I was working in Sector 23 for the last ten years, but I got transferred two weeks ago. I was the foreman on the new turbine installation project. That's why I wanted to talk to you."

"Look, I'm sorry you got transferred but I don't have anything to do with that sort of stuff. You can just forget my using any influence to help you get back to working with your buddies and old cronies...," began Jim.

"Hey! I set this meeting, not you," interrupted John sternly. "I only have a little bit of time. It is very important that you just listen!"

"How did you get this meeting set in the first place?" asked Jim, caught off guard. Something in the man's voice told him he had better listen.

"I had someone tap into your schedule in the computer. I knew you wouldn't see me. This is important sir, so please, I need for you to hear me out."

John took a deep breath and began again. "There is something terrible about to happen here. You see, I have worked for this company most of my life. I have seen things change for us, mostly taking things away little by little, but on the whole this place has been very fair to me."

"Sir, something happened two weeks ago that you won't believe. We were working on that new turbine project. We were tunneling for a deep underground installation in the west area. The whole thing is just terrible. Four guys were working in the shaft when, all of a sudden, we lost voice contact with the team leader."

Jim felt a hot heaviness in his solar plexus. He was bright enough to see the connection to his meeting with Jackson and the dreadful news he was sure was coming.

John took a drink of his water. "Anyway, the crew down below just quit responding to the top side, so we put emergency rescue procedures into action. We lowered a team into the tunnel equipped with gas protection and full rescue support. I was on that team. Those were my men down there."

"When we got to the bottom," he paused, clenching his jaw for a moment, "it was horrible. The men were on their sides or face down, vomiting and choking. They were being poisoned to death by ammonia gas. Have you ever seen anybody die like that, sir?" questioned John.

Jim flashed back to a movie he had seen recently about the Nazi death camps. It had been one of those stark reality films made in black and white for effect. They had shown the panic of the prisoners as the gas poured from the shower heads. The people had clawed the doors like animals in terror and pain.

"They didn't die right away, sir," said John, bring-

The Office

ing Jim back, "but it would have been better if they had. Their lungs were seared so badly that three of them could not survive. The fourth man is in the hospital now, but he is in a coma and will probably die soon."

"We have spent tons of money on safety equipment, gas detectors, and precautions in this last year alone," blurted out Jim defensively. "There hasn't been a serious accident in this sector in three years and there hasn't been a death here for ten. What went wrong?"

"The safety equipment that was required for this job, and was supposed to be in place before we ever began installation, was faked!" shot back John.

"Faked?" echoed Jim, weakly.

"Yeah, they stuck some boxes down there to make it look like the place was protected, but when they were checked after the accident they were only imitations," explained John. "Someone deliberately put in phony safety equipment to save a buck and it cost the lives of some very good men. Real people, not numbers on a payroll sheet.

These men had families and hopes and dreams. Some idiot thought he'd trim his bottom line. Whoever did this ought to be sent straight to hell!" John's face was red. Veins in his neck began to pulse as he stared angrily at Jim.

"Why are you telling me this?" asked Jim, now obviously uncomfortable.

John leaned forward and spoke softly but angrily,

his eyes fixed on Jim. "Because someone in Sector 23, your sector, is trying to cover up the whole thing and blame it on the leader of the drilling team!"

"What do you mean?"

"Listen, I may be only a worker at the bottom of the barrel here, but when you have been around as long as I have, you hear things. The word is out that someone is going to make it look as though someone made a deal with the foreman, that's me installed those fake boxes, and stole the money," continued John. "If that happens, I will go to jail with someone up there, maybe you! My life will be destroyed, sir. Just like those men in that tunnel!"

Jim sat stunned, suddenly aware that something like this was possible. This is what Jackson meant by "putting it down the line." Of course, executive privilege, well connected veterans, had the power to create a bogus paper trail. They could paint the picture any way they pleased and no one could ever unravel the truth. Jim knew how easily it could be done.

"I want to show you something," John spoke quietly. He pulled out an old wallet and turned to a set of flip-over pictures. Stopping at a family portrait he announced, "This is my wife, Suzie, and these are my two girls. We've been married 27 years and the youngest girl, my Angie, she will be a sophomore at City College next year. Her sister, April, will be a senior. Angie wants to go to medical school and it takes every dime I've got to keep her going. But she is a great kid

The Office

and will make a fantastic doctor one day."

Jim looked at the picture. It was a department store cheapie. One of those that gets you in for a few bucks, takes dozens of shots, and then tries to sell you the rest when you come back. Though the picture was basic, the family was not. John looked out of place in his cheap brown suit and out of style tie, but they sure looked like they all loved each other. He thought about the picture in his own wallet. John had a genuine family, thought Jim.

John was looking at the pictures, too, not at Jim. He flipped to another set of photos. "This is my little sister, Doris, and her husband, Arthur."

Jim looked impatiently at the picture and was about to interrupt when John said, "Arthur died at the bottom of that shaft. You see, sir, I'm responsible for his family now. I could never have done anything to hurt those men. My own brother-in-law was down there. I had to watch Arthur die! Worse than any amount of money or jail for a crime I did not commit would be the possibility that some big-wig would make it look like I killed my own little sister's husband."

Jim wondered if his own family would believe the company over him? Could the power and credibility of the corporation extend that far? He stared at the foreman and his dirty overalls.

"Please, sir, you have got to help me," pleaded John.

"What in the world do you expect me to do?" asked Jim sarcastically.

"You can talk to people I can't. You can even report to Mr. Flint. If you'll help me, you can save me. If you won't, there is no telling what will happen to me, my family, and my sister and her kids," begged John, his tough face filling with tears. "Please, please don't let this happen to all these people. Don't let this happen to me!" The man took hold of Jim's forearm. His strong fingers hurt as they squeezed tightly. The pain on John's face tore into Jim.

"Okay, okay, I'll see what I can do," agreed Jim, trying to get the man to let go of his arm.

"Thank you, thank you, so much, sir. Here's my phone number and address," John said, handing Jim a folded yellow flyer with a name and number scrawled across it in blue ink. "Thank you, thank you, and God bless you and your family!"

Jim watched as John from Sector 6 walked quickly out of the cafeteria. He had barely touched the sandwich on his tray. Jim quickly ate his strawberry shortcake and took his fractured company conscience back to his office. He was totally confused.

That had begun three sleepless nights. Friday came. The painful confrontation with his boss and Mr. Flint still sent bolts of nervous lightning through his stomach as he heard their angry words. Jim took the high ground and appealed to them to do the right thing. His boss came at him like a wounded animal ready to tear him to pieces. In the end, Jim learned that his boss and Flint had actually embezzled the money and were prepared to pin it on Jim if he did not sign the forms that would implicate John, the foreman. They were going to get away with it and there was nothing he could do.

Fearfully he agonized over the decision. The report he has seen contained photographs of the disaster. The pictures of the horror John had witnessed first hand. The images burned in his mind. Finally, a prisoner of his own conscience, he could not remain silent. Surprising even himself, Jim decided to report the truth. It cost him everything.

THE PARK

The cool, green grass of the City Park rolled gently down to a duck pond. The bluish-green coolness of the water looked so peaceful and lovely.

It couldn't be very deep though, since it was a small park and all, Jim thought as he watched a woman with a baby in a stroller and a toddler feeding stale bread to the black ducks. The woman was carefully tending her toddler and the stroller at the same time in that deft, but natural way mothers do.

Jim sat back on the wood and wrought iron park bench. He rubbed the dry roughness of the wood between his thumb and forefinger as he looked back down the hill. He placed his scheduling planner and the book he was trying to read beside him, turning them with their spine to the breeze so they would not fly open.

"Fired!" Jim still recoiled from the sting of the idea. Fired! The anger came again. "It was them all along, but I get fired!" he gritted to himself angrily through clenched teeth.

That had been almost two weeks ago. He replayed the scenes that had built to the crazy outcome one more time in his mind, looking for understanding. The powerful executives were able to turn the tables and make it look as if Jim were to blame. They produced false documents with Jim's signature authorizing the dummy equipment. They offered Jim a "deal."

If he took the blame quietly, he would lose his job, but they would give him full pay and benefits for one year. Cooperate and the company would not press charges. If he went to court they would fight tooth and nail with all the money and power of the corporation behind them. Jim's attorney told him it would cost a fortune, take years, and be almost impossible to win. Some deal.

It was worse than a nightmare. Jim signed the papers, cleared out his desk, shipped his personal belongings to his home and was escorted out the door by a security guard in humiliation. He could still feel the stares of his co-workers as they watched him walk the gauntlet to the lobby with his eyes on his shoes, his tallness embarrassingly obvious.

They had recruited him right out of college. He had worked for the company his entire adult life. The whole world was out of focus and everything he had ever believed in was upside down.

Compounding the crisis, his wife and children had all but kicked him out of the house. They were treating him like a criminal, and Tracey actually had the nerve to insinuate that perhaps the company report was true.

Maybe Jim really was the incompetent one who let

those men die, she had said coldly, doubting his story. Jim's heart raced as he felt again the anguish of the bitter words. He saw the moment again. There she was, hands on her hips. Her eyes revealed confusion and the hurt she, too, was feeling. He wanted to hold her, but instead had given a choked, desperate laugh, and walked away.

The lack of love in their marriage was a ready garden where the seeds of doubt and anger could now grow wildly. She was a stock broker who earned more money than he did. It made Jim uncomfortable, but they only spoke about it in teasing comments, usually with other couples at parties where he laughed along. Now the unspoken tensions of the years were full blown nightmares he was having every night. They had been sleeping in separate rooms and he often awoke in a sweating terror. Even the dreadful and scary tiger dream he used to have as a child had returned. He was a ghost in his own house, silent and defeated.

Jim opened his wallet and looked at the picture. It had been taken a couple of years ago at a ski vacation. It was a rare moment they shared together and Jim remembered it fondly as one of the happiest times in his life. His pretty wife was tall and athletic. She used to laugh and say she liked Jim because she was a big girl and felt awkward with men shorter than her. That always made him feel great!

His daughter, Claire, was also athletic and active. She had inherited his wife's dark hair and green eyes.

Sure to get a scholarship, she excelled on all the sports teams at her high school. They were close when she was little, but she was so popular and busy now he felt like he hardly knew her anymore. She was so different now from the smiling child he saw in the photo.

His son was another matter. Roger was a smart-aleck with a high IQ but would score very low on a personality test. He loved to correct everyone. To Roger, tact was a nasty, four letter word to be avoided. The sandy haired, freckle-faced little nerd would probably live at home with Jim and Tracey forever. Jim thought how little time he had spent with Roger when he was a small boy, and even less now. Perhaps more "Dad" would have made a difference in the boy's life.

They sure looked good in this picture though. Kind of like an ad in a travel magazine. He had assumed the lack of communication was natural teenage growing pains. After being around the house for several days it was obvious they were taking Tracey's side in the blame game.

"People somehow seemed happier in those vacation pictures," he mused. He looked at the people in the picture and felt like they were strangers in someone else's wallet.

He gazed down the hill toward the duck pond and tried to imagine his future. It was completely blank. Even his imagination seemed to be broken. It was one thing to have a mid-life crisis and buy a new wardrobe, a sports car, then start thinking about

The Park

leaving your wife for the new receptionist. It was another thing altogether to go to bed quietly, safe and snug, then wake up in the middle of the wilderness!

That's how he saw his life. There was nothing there but miles of confusion and he doubted his own ability to hike out. Was he really this weak and foolish? Would he simply die out here? His old fears and doubts attacked in waves and painted mental pictures of the worst outcomes. The seminar he had attended had called it "awfulizing." He knew it, but couldn't seem to pull out.

Jim turned sideways on the bench to prop his feet up and knocked his day-planner off onto the ground. Several papers slid out onto the freshly mowed grass. The wind instantly noticed and began to scatter them across the park. He half-chuckled wearily as he bent to retrieve his past life.

"I don't know why I even bother to carry this darn thing around," he wondered aloud. "I haven't written anything in it in two weeks, and I sure don't have any appointments to keep."

A bright yellow flyer had drifted farther away than the others. It was caught and fluttering on a hedge like a small bird struggling to be free and fly away on a gust of wind. Jim snatched it up. It was the telephone number John from Sector Six had given him.

He wondered if John knew about all that had happened. Jim had been too blown away by the events to call him. Turning the paper over he realized John had written his number on the back of an advertisement for the Safari Adventure Company. A thousand thoughts rushed through his head as he remembered his visit and Benjamin, the fascinating Australian. John must have taken it off the bulletin board at work.

The park trash can was a few steps away. Jim walked over to clean out the scraps of paper from the planner. Tossing the debris into the can, he hesitated over the brochure. He looked dreamily at the scenes of elephants, birds, and smiling men and women. Jim imagined wearing the cool bush hat on the head of the man on the front of the brochure. Sighing, he slowly released it and let it sink into the bottom of the empty green barrel.

It's probably just some bored, old timers riding around in a jeep wearing designer bush-wear. I'll bet there's a staff photographer who'll sell you back your memories at the clubhouse later, over a few ales, he thought bitterly. Sadly, in real life, nobody ever delivers. The real thing never looks as good as the brochures.

Jim walked in slow motion back to the bench and sat down wearily. He felt as though all the energy was drained from his life. Clearing his throat, he wondered if be might be coming down with some kind of cold.

He looked back down the hill at the duck pond. Another mini-tribe had arrived. Jim watched as the mother tied the shoe of a very active boy and gave him important instructions. She then turned and be-

The Park

gan tending and talking to her stroller passenger. The boy soon began inching his way toward the pond while carefully watching to see if mom was looking.

Reaching the edge, he spied a duck who had come to the edge of the pond to mooch for bread. Removing his freshly tied shoes and clean white cotton socks, he stood and surveyed the situation. He looked first at the duck, then back at his mother. In one quick motion he turned and lowered himself backward down the little cement bank and into the six inches of water at the edge.

Smiling a mischievous smile, eyes wide, he stepped softly toward the trusting duck, his extended hand clinching make-believe bread. The duck floated closer. Suddenly, the duck realized there was no bread. It was a trap instead! It honked loudly, beat the water with its wings, and paddled backwards furiously.

In the flurry and noise the duck splashed and soaked the youngster who covered his face with his hands and squealed with total ecstasy at the sight and sensation!

"WILLIAM JASON ANDERSON!" screamed his mother, as she spun around and reached the pond instantly. Swooping the hunter up with one arm and swatting his behind in one seamless motion, she recited what must have been a "greatest hits" selection for the boy.

"How many times have I told you to stay out of that pond?" she asked, expecting no real number for an answer. She scolded and dried him with extra verses of future warnings. Eventually the young explorer was hugging her, swearing his love, and apologizing. They embraced as she kissed his damp head. Soon he was swinging on the swingset, a duck feather squeezed tightly in his hand, the trophy of the mighty deed.

Well, there it was. William Jason Anderson knew the price he would pay for taking the risk. The call of adventure was stronger than the voice of fear. On the shore was predictable safety, but out in the pond was possibility. The boy had guts.

Jim sat and watched in silence.

Where does the courage go? He wondered. When does the spirit and passion for life you had as a youth start to slowly go dim and ebb into complacent, predictable, adult scorekeeping? His heart ached. He could almost feel the nothingness sliding through his outstretched fingers. He needed a reason, a purpose, something! Even something to fight! Something he could hit and hurt and defeat! But all he had was a hollow wanting.

The mother was now chasing the shrieking youngster in play. Her smile and mock threats of tickling were so full of love as she maneuvered, out of breath, around the monkey bars. Her baby grinned a broad toothless grin from its box seat, tucked safely in one of her arms. After the family played a while, they wandered around to the concession stand for ice cream and over the hill toward the parking area.

The Park

Jim sat staring into the trees for a long time. Then he gathered up his belongings and walked slowly to the trash can. He looked around to make sure no one else could see him, then he bent over and reached all the way into the nearly empty barrel. He pulled out the brochure, stuffed it into his pocket, and walked hopefully toward his car.

"Jackson and Flint can go to hell!" he said out loud. "I am going to Africa!"

AFRICA

The incredibly dense and lush tropical jungle was dark and scary. The closeness of the bush was made even more suffocating by the crawling insects and slithering reptiles that seemed to be everywhere. Jim was frozen with terror. His arms and legs were too heavy to lift. The eyes of an enormous tiger were fixed on his own eyes. Jim knew that if he moved the wrong way the tiger would leap once and sink its teeth deep into his throat, then rip away savagely, tearing the jugular and executing him like a professional assassin.

Except for the tip of its tail moving hypnotically like a charmed cobra, the tiger was absolutely still. It had killed many times before and its primitive instinct was ready to eat. The shocking orange and black markings, so attractive behind the cage bars in the zoo, were now a flash of terror. The beast turned suddenly as a blue parrot flushed from the bush to Jim's right. In sheer panic Jim turned to run. Out of the corner of his eye he saw, as if in slow motion, the tiger explode off the ground and head directly on a course to intercept him. He screamed.

Jim sat bolt upright and looked around the plane

to see if others had heard him cry out. He was sweating despite the cool overhead fan. He first had the tiger dream as a young boy. Then again in college. It had gone away after he got married, but recently it had returned to his nightmares. The dream had almost kept him from going to Africa. He had been quite comforted by the television program he had seen last week that assured him tigers were Asian creatures and there were none in Africa.

Turning toward the window, he saw the sparkling vastness of the Atlantic Ocean splashed against the pearl white sand of the Western coast of Africa. He had awakened just in time to be the first to see land. With his nose pressed against the window of the jet liner, Jim watched as the small strip of sand immediately slid under the emerald canopy of an endless jungle. No photograph, no video, no description from a podium could begin to embrace the power and size of the land once called the dark continent. Jim marveled at the thought of the European explorers who had crossed it on foot to map and learn of its mysteries so long ago.

He sat back in his seat after his neck grew sore from twisting to see it all. It would be several hours before they reached Johannesburg. There they would catch a shuttle plane to Lilongwe International Airport, in southern Malawi. The man in the seat beside him was fast asleep. A freckled nose was all that was visible beneath the blanket pulled over his face.

When he had told Tracey he was going to go on

Africa

the Safari, she had barely cared. She told him it would be fine with her if he would just get out of the house for a while. He had faintly hoped she would express some concern that she might miss him, but there was no hint of that in her voice at all. When he had asked foolishly if she hated him, she replied, "The opposite of love is not hate, it's apathy, remember?"

He had once said the same thing to an employee at work. The young secretary had asked his opinion about a boyfriend for whom she had lost interest. He had imagined himself so clever then, he had told Tracey about his advice that evening. Now the words rang true in his own life. She just didn't care anymore. The kids had nothing to say. Their silence said much more.

The flight seemed to last forever. Jim sat and re-read the letter Tracey had placed in his travel bag before he had departed. She said he was insensitive. That he had hurt her over and over with his critical words. He had made her feel stupid and unloved. How interesting, he thought. He felt as though she were the stronger in the relationship. This sure did not sound like the attractive, confident stockbroker who had made better grades in school and earned so much money.

She accused him of being a poor father. This really stung. He worked hard to be successful, but successful at what? Immersed in his work he had sacrificed spending time with his growing children to make the late meetings that dragged on at work or a club.

What were his peers' personal lives like? Jim had always assumed that the huge sums of money they made would surely heal any temporary separation from their families. He opened his wallet and looked at the picture from the ski resort again. He looked at the letter. He stared out the window.

His daydream was interrupted by the voice of the captain announcing their descent into the airport. The shift in thought gave Jim a shot of excitement. Andy stretched and returned to the land of the living with a huge yawn.

"Are we there yet, Daddy?" he kidded Jim.

Andy was a lot of fun to be around. He was in his late 30's with shocking red hair, a slim build, and a non-stop grin. There was no topic that was safe from the ravages of his hilarious one-liners. Jim liked the red headed jokester. Andy had three girls and worked as a salesman for a document and label manufacturer. He confided to Jim that the Safari Adventure Company was subsidizing his trip by continuing to pay his salary and bonus to his wife and girls, so he was able to attend.

Like Jim, Andy had been handed a piece of paper about the Safari and had contacted Benjamin on a lark. It was a tough decision for him to be gone for long. He dearly loved his daughters and was already a bit homesick, though he wouldn't admit it. Andy was using the time to reflect and to try to learn more about himself. He hoped the safari would bring something out in his life that had seemingly died. They had a lot of laughs on the flight and were beginning to build a friendship as they shared stories on the long flight over the ocean.

The plane descended into a surprisingly modern airport. The group stayed together and stretched their legs while their bags were loaded on to the shuttle plane. Smiles were all around. Though a little weary from the long flight, they were troopers and kept a positive attitude. Benjamin gently guided them with affirmations of what was next at each juncture.

The flight to Lilongwe, capital of Malawi, was short and easy. As they walked down the ramp, their bags were loaded into two Land Rovers by uniformed attendants. There were 5 passengers in each jeep. Andy and Jim were in one and Benjamin joined the crew in the other.

The jeeps rolled along through the edge of town. In the distance the capital city could be seen. Its 1960s style office buildings, cathedrals, and white frame houses stood out as a stark contrast to the African landscape and the mountains in the distance. They traveled along increasingly rougher roads as they headed southwest through the southern end of the great Rift Valley.

The countryside was alive with gold and brown grass fields that stretched seemingly forever, alternating with patches of forests, scrub, and underbrush. They had only been on the road for about half an hour when they spotted a large herd of Nyala, a large graceful antelope. There were hundreds of the bright orange, black and tan creatures who sprang majestically, taking huge strides. With each leap their majestic horns (should he call them antlers?) long and straight like a pair of unicorn swords pointed to the sky with regal and primitive beauty.

"My name is Kamuto!" announced the driver. He was in his mid-20s, smiling and looking dapper in his gold and black chauffeur hat and Colorado Rockies T-shirt. He lived in Lilongwe and owned his own Land Rover. The idea of owning your own business was new and exciting for him. The recently deposed "President for Life," His Excellency Dr. Bandu, had restricted such activity, and Kamuto to was very proud of his entrepreneurship.

He passed a water bottle around the cab, and everyone realized how very thirsty they were.

"Hey! Don't drink too much!" He shouted to the group with a big, toothy smile. "I'm not stopping every five minutes for you kids to go to the bathroom!" he kidded good naturedly with his British accent.

Andy laughed heartily and smiled across the jeep at Jim. Then he began telling jokes to the driver who was a fresh and willing victim for Andy's favorites. They were laughing at regular intervals only stopping for Andy to repeat the joke so the driver could tell it later and laughing at it all over again.

Africa

Jim smiled, too. Everyone was looking out the windows—their thoughts arriving and departing at 200 miles per hour. A monkey scooted up a tree as the jeep approached.

After an hour or so, they stopped at a road side fruit stand. There they stocked up on delicious mangoes, bananas, and pineapples. The mangoes cost less than one African cent! As they pressed on, they saw more and more wildlife including endless birds of beautiful color and plumage and many different breeds of antelope.

"Look there!" called Kamuto, pointing out his window, "there in the distance."

Everyone stopped chatting and looked to see three elephants standing near a clump of acacia trees. "Oohs" and "aahs" were everywhere as suddenly more than a dozen giraffes walked out of the trees just a few hundred meters from the elephants. "Now you have officially been welcomed to Africa!" announced Kamuto loudly. "You have seen elephants!"

Finally, they arrived at the lodge. The Kudya Discovery Lodge was just outside the Liwonde National Park. It was an enormous and picturesque place. The wide porch wrapped all the way around the building and was lined with wicker chairs and little teakwood coffee tables. You could practically hear the tall tales that must have been spun here by courageous pioneers and eccentric adventurers.

Everyone thanked Kamuto and bid him farewell as

they gathered their bags, happy to be anywhere, at last. Jim and Andy bounded up the steps and crossed the porch eagerly. As soon as they entered the already open doors, they stopped to take in the panorama of excited activity. There must have been fifty people talking and gesturing excitedly as they shared stories and introductions. Smiles and laughter were everywhere. Those that were not in groups were moving up and down the staircases that bordered the high ceilinged great room on either side. It was an absolute museum.

There were trophy heads of every conceivable creature lining the walls. African shields, spears, ornate feathered masks, pipes and tribal vesture pervaded every surface. More treasures even hung majestically from the huge, bare rafters overhead. Everywhere space allowed, a photograph of some past adventure was squeezed in. The pictures were amazing. As Jim looked more closely, he could see that the obviously modern, color, friendlier poses replaced the stern, masculine ones that reached as far back as the previous century. Across the room to the left was an enormous front desk staffed by clerks attired in bright red uniforms checking in the last arrivals.

"Mister Jim, you are very welcome here," beamed the English accented African clerk after Jim introduced himself. "You will be staying in room number two-hundred seventeen.

"Who is my roommate?" asked Jim.

"A Mister Weinberg it seems, sir."

Africa

Jim tried to imagine what a Weinberg might look like. While Andy was getting his room assignment, Jim turned and caught a glimpse of himself in the gigantic mirror right next to the bell stand. He studied himself carefully at first, pulling his bush jacket up a bit and tugging up his fatigue pants.

"Hey," he thought adjusting his cool hat, " I don't look too bad!"

When he caught himself smiling at the man in the mirror, he laughed out loud. It was such a happy laugh and felt so good he just closed his eyes and let it go. He then realized what he was doing and sobered up quickly, looking around to see if anyone was staring. They weren't. They were all too caught up in their personal excitement to single out one of their own as peculiar! When was the last time he laughed like that? He turned back to the desk clerk, still grinning.

"OK, 217. Here's your key, Mister Jim. You may want to freshen up first. Dinner will be from 6 p.m. until 10 p.m.," smiled the cheerful clerk.

"Four hours for dinner?" questioned Jim. "Why so long?"

Benjamin stepped up to his side and answered. "Jim, there's a lot of dinner, and much to tell. You will be hearin' stories from some of the old timers of the Club," he explained. He leaned closer to Jim and whispered, "You will hear things tonight that could only happen in Africa!"

Benjamin had walked up as Jim turned to pick up his bags. He was in the company of an athletic young woman in her mid 30's who looked like she was not a happy camper. They had been introduced to Karin on the plane. She had gotten into at least two arguments with the hostess over the food and the in-flight movie. She was an interesting study with her light brown hair in a ponytail and her designer shorts, shirt, and hat with matching luggage. She looked like she had been a cheerleader in college and was very attractive. Her beauty, however, was overshadowed by a foul disposition.

"What a terrible flight!" was her opening remark. "The ride in those awful jeeps was worse, though. I think our driver hit every rock, pothole, and monkey skull between the airport and the gate!"

"What kind of spider is that in your hair?" asked Andy, reaching toward the top of her head.

"Aaaaggghhh!" screamed Karin slapping her head like Curly of the 3 Stooges. "Get'em off me, get'em off me!"

Andy burst out in laughter as the others smiled to realize he was only joking. Karin socked him in the shoulder and gave him the most unapproving look she had.

They all shook hands and agreed to meet downstairs later before dinner and headed off to their rooms. Jim made his way to the second floor room admiring the sights and atmosphere of the place all the way.

Africa

Placing his bags on the empty bed, he checked out the luggage of his roommate—black leather and very expensive. A worn copy of The Three Treasures lay on the night stand. Jim picked it up carefully. Turning the cover, he read the inscription:

> *To my dearest companion, Weinberg. May your life run to overflowing with these priceless treasures and may you have the boundless joy of giving them away to someone else as I have done with you.*
> — *Colonel Hampton Featherwood, 1966*

The sound of the turning key caught Jim by surprise. He quickly replaced the book on the nightstand and turned to face the opening door. In walked Weinberg. He was in his late fifties, but exceptionally fit and healthy. In fact, he practically glowed. He had a medium build and charcoal gray hair. One thing that really stood out were his dark, piercing eyes. They looked as if they could see right through you and into your soul. Not in a spooky way, but see someone for who they really are. Jim liked him before a word was spoken.

A warm gentle voice with a slight English accent brought power and dignity to the simple words, "Jim, it's so very wonderful to meet you!"

"Thanks, great to be here!" Trying not to be awkwardly formal, Jim asked, "What shall I call you, Sir?"

"Weinberg, of course," he answered giving Jim a wink and a silly thumbs up.

The two took an immediate liking to one another. Weinberg told Jim that he had been in camp for four days preparing for the safari. He explained that he was a long time member of the club and would be on one of the teams as a fellow hiker.

"The safari uses a smashing concept," Weinberg said, excitedly. "We pair up green peas—oh, forgive me, that is what we call first time hikers!—anyway, we partner up newcomers and veterans. This gives us all a chance to meet new people and share ideas. I will be happy to be your personal guide!"

"That will be great!" said Jim.

"There will be a banquet tonight. You are in for a real treat! Then you will rest up from the jet lag and all. There will be a bit of an orientation tomorrow afternoon, then off we go!" Weinberg continued.

Jim was glad to hear about the rest time. He was already feeling a little fatigued from the flight, but the adrenaline was pumping from the fascinating atmosphere and excitement of it all.

After they had talked for quite some time, Weinberg suggested they go to the overlook for the show.

"Show? What show?" asked Jim.

"Oh, yes, I have forgotten this is your first time here. Every evening, just near sunset, an entire herd of hippos comes out to graze on the lawns of the lodge. It is a sight you simply must not miss!"

HEROES AND LEGENDS

Weinberg was right, it was an amazing experience to witness these monstrous creatures graze gently like cattle. Jim had seen hippos only in the movies, covered up to their eyeballs in water. The mother and baby won the adoration of the group, who sat in hushed appreciation at the south end of the porch.

As the sunset turned from scarlet to bronze, little gas-lights were lit all around the area by the staff. They left the porch and were instantly hailed by a group of adventurers seated just inside the dining room. "Weinberg!" the group called out in unison, then burst into laughter at their chorus. Weinberg responded loudly, "Hello, you bush babies!" giving his signature wink and thumbs up. "I want you to meet my new friend and first time safari man, Jim." Weinberg announced proudly as if Jim were one of his closest and dearest friends. The whole group stood politely and greeted Jim as if he were the Prince of Wales.

There was a Dutchman in a tuxedo. An American from Detroit who shook Jim's hand firmly and told him how fortunate he was to be rooming with Weinberg. The others agreed with vigorous nods and "you bet's". A young Japanese man was introduced as a "first tripper" escorted by an older friend from his home town.

The obvious leader and elder statesman of the group was Edward Pennybrook. He must have been nearly eighty, but his energy and gusto masked the fact. They all deferred to Pennybrook whenever opinions were given and never crossed words with him, but nodded thoughtfully instead. But there was little seriousness tonight. They were old friends catching up on jokes and Pennybrook was in the thick of it. He started by lowering his voice, to draw them in, and began;

"A man was driving through the countryside in rural America when he noticed a farmer holding a pig up to a cornstalk as the pig ate from it. The man thought this was very unusual so he pulled his vehicle to the side and rolled down the glass. "Hello, my dear fellow! Wouldn't it save some time to throw the corn on the ground?" he asked. The farmer looked up and frowned at the man. He said, "You city fellows are so dumb! What's time to a pig!"

The group erupted in glee and howled with laughter. Pennybrook laughed harder than anyone at his own joke and then fell into a coughing and gasping fit that set the whole group off again.

"Pennybrook, tell the monkey and the piano again!" shouted the Dutchman after Pennybrook had stopped coughing.

"Lad, I just told it a moment ago, didn't I?" questioned Pennybrook with false modesty.

"Yes, yes, you did, but Weinberg and Sir Jim were not here," he reminded.

"Tell it again, tell it again!" egged on the others enthusiastically.

Pennybrook was in heaven. He leaned back and made a very serious face.

"Once I walked into a pub in Southampton and sat at the bar and ordered an ale," he began quite factually. "Over in the corner there was a man happily playing the piano although there were only a couple of patrons in the whole of the place. Interestingly enough there was a monkey sitting on top of the piano wearing a little suit and derby that matched that of the piano man. The bartender brought the ale, but as I reached for it the monkey jumped down from the piano, ran over and leaped up on the bar, drank my beer right down, wiped his mouth on his sleeve and slammed the mug back on the bar.

It happened so frightfully fast that no one else saw it. Before I could say a bloody word the monkey was sitting back on the piano as if nothin' happened. I didn't want to raise a row so I just ordered another ale. Before I could get to it again the monkey came and did the very same thing!"

Jim was already laughing as the Englishman made a pantomime of the dramatic way the monkey wiped his mouth and slammed the mug to the bar. The group was in ecstasy and laughed all the harder for having heard the joke already.

"Still, not being from around these parts, I orders one more beer. The little booger beat me to it again and actually stared at me after he finished my ale and seemed to be daring me to do anythin'. So I walks over to the piano player—he's playin' away—and taps him on the shoulder. He looks up and smiles and says, Hullo, mate, what can I do for you?'

I says to him. Excuse me, Bub, but do you know your monkey drank my beer?'

He smiled back at me and said, Don't think I do, but if you hum a few bars I'll bet I can fake it!'"

Another explosion of laughter rocked the table, and one of the men spilled his drink in his lap and ran off to the rest room to regroup. The others repeated, "Do you know your monkey drank my beer?" over and over as they slapped each other on the back and howled.

Jim laughed along with the ancient jokes. He had heard them long ago as a child, but it didn't seem to matter tonight. Pennybrook continued to preside over the group until they were joined by a tall, elegant, blonde German lady named Nina. Though she, too, wore safari clothes, she somehow affected a European elegance.

She was in her later 50s and instantly stole the spotlight with her charm and stories of the European Safari Company she had helped operate in West Berlin for the last 20 years. Nina was so well read and educated that the entire level of sophistication went up 100% in the group when she joined them. Jim was very impressed by the class shown by the group and their versatility in conversation.

Soon however she caught them all off guard with a sharply funny joke about the American President that sent the group into a controlled giggle, and then they were off again with the fun. This continued through a sumptuous dinner of exotic foods that came in multiple courses of small, but delicious portions. Jim enjoyed himself immensely, but only after proper identification of the ingredients!

As coffee was being served, Jim noticed some people had gathered on the riser at the center of the hall. Three men and the German lady, Nina, were seated in large wicker rattan chairs facing the group. The man at the microphone must have been the oldest man in the room. His massive swirl of cotton white hair made him look like Einstein with a beard. He was dressed in an off white linen suit with a bright purple African flower in the lapel. Looking out over the happily chatting people with some satisfaction, he smiled and cleared his throat intentionally, calling the group to order.

"Ladies and gentlemen," he began in grand ballroom style. His deep rich bass voice made you want to immediately sit up straight in your chair.

"I now call to order this gathering of the Royal Safari Adventure Company Society. Welcome, and most gracious regards to our honored guests and members. We are positively thrilled to host your attendance at this most formal occasion!" At the word "formal" his eyebrows and the corners of his mouth went straight up. He swept his upturned hand in a presentation gesture toward the only person clad in a tuxedo, the elegant Dutchman. The Dutchman stood and bowed in majestic fashion. The audience laughed warmly at their dear friend who enjoyed surprising everyone whenever possible. At his bow the laughter turned into applause.

We especially want to recognize our first time adventurers. Will all the people making their first ever safari please stand. Jim slowly stood self-consciously and was joined by about twenty others. He looked for his American teammates and saw Andy across the room, seated next to Benjamin. Andy smiled broadly and made one of the funniest faces possible. Jim beamed back as the veteran members cheered wildly, encouraging the newcomers. It was an exhilarating feeling to be here in the company of such incredible people!

Jim and the others sat down quickly and the speaker began again.

"My name is Arthur Kipper and I have been a member of the Club for 65 years. Two months ago I celebrated my 91st birthday, and I had considered foregoing this trip because of my age. Others phoned and convinced me not to let my youth detain me!

Weinberg, in fact, said that if I stayed at home, the Americans would call me a, weenie.' Would someone please tell me what that means?"

The audience showed their love with applause and cheers.

"Now that I am here among my dearest friends, I am thrilled to touch the wood on the banister of the old staircase, to see the photographs I have loved since my youth, to smell the air and flowers again. Here the years melt away. My friends, if you are granted the grace of a long life such as I have had, you will one day understand what it feels like to have the heart of a youth in the body of a seasoned citizen!

"It is long ago, yet it seems only recently that I sat in this hall, like many of you here for the first time tonight; a green pea. I was brand new, excited, nervous and quite in awe of the men and women that surrounded me here. That night there were people in this room that had seen things we read about only in books today. With their own eyes they saw new worlds. They forged history with their own hands. Men and women who had explored this country long before there was technology to make them safe.

"There sat people who had accompanied Amundson and Perry to the poles of the globe. At my table were Albert Schweitzer and Stanley Livingstone's companions, and still others who had fought in the American Civil War. People who had lived lives so far beyond the average... my friends, their names will never be in the history books because they were behind the scenes, doing it! But, they were real heroes!

"There I sat, a wet-nosed lad, wondering why these extraordinary people would take the time to take us on safari. There would be no money, no property, no fame, but, there would indeed be treasure! They came to give back to this noble effort. They gave their time, their hearts, their talents, to this timeless chain. They were passing the torch of the one true light that has come into the world, and we are here to pass that same light on to these men and women who have come here just like you and I!"

The crowd erupted in spontaneous applause. Standing as one, they thrust their fists into the air and shouted their approval. Stepping back from the microphone, the elder statesman joined them by shoving his arms aloft and smiling broadly. After a moment, he returned to the podium and continued, "But it is not like me to be so wordy." The crowd chuckled. "I want to introduce to you now, some people who will share their wisdom and perhaps, if we are fortunate, a tale or two about the safari ahead."

First, he invited to the podium an oriental twig of a man named Songh Singh. He began with a joke about his name. Jim was fascinated as he shared the view of an Eastern man about the wonder and beauty of Africa.

"The ancient proverb says that as iron sharpens iron, so one friend sharpens another," he said. "I am referring to my deep appreciation for the honor of sharing my life with some of the members of this company. It is said that we are becoming the average of our 5 closest associates in life. If that is true, and I believe it is, you could do no better than the people here tonight.

The power of nature and physical exertion, blended with these friendships, have been the garden in which I have found spiritual enlightenment. This understanding has been a light on my path, an internal compass that shows me which way to go when there are no maps."

"You see," he continued thoughtfully, "my life was once very tedious and without meaning. My marriage was bitter and filled with constant disagreement and misunderstanding. I believed all my problems were caused by the external influences in my life. The government, the work, my wife, my parents, my customers were all my antagonists. I used to say, 'All my problems talk back!' Then, my dear friend taught me to understand The Three Treasures." With this he turned and bowed to the sandy haired American man on the platform. The man wore a Cleveland Indians baseball jacket and jeans. He looked to be in his late 50s, and was ruddy and tanned. His face looked like leather, but his eyes were clear and bright. He nodded back gracefully.

"The Three Treasures' were only a beginning. They started me on a mighty journey, no, an adventure, that powers my life even to this day. After the safari, I set goals for my life for the very first time. You who are new must ask yourself what you want your life to look like in five years. Have you ever done this?

"You see, my father was a fisherman. His father was a fisherman. His father before him was a fisherman. It was always understood that Songh Singh would be a fisherman, too. There was just one problem—I hated fish! My friend heard me complaining about my dilemma and said to me, Songh, you are not a duck! You are not one of God's machines.' He showed me that the duck must fly north for the summer and south for the winter. Without exception, his fate, his destiny, is set in stone. You, however, can go in any direction you choose. In fact, the only reason your life does not change is if you choose to keep it the same.

"I realized that the influences that I thought were controlling my life were only doing so because of my permission! I took control of my destiny and set new goals. You see, I had always been fascinated by electronics. I worked hard and went to school at night to learn what I loved. I read books, I apprenticed for free at repair businesses and eventually I got a new job in the business I loved. I then set new goals to own a business, and now I do own a rather modest copier company."

Weinberg elbowed Jim, "Modest? Songh is worth millions!" he said. "His company is not in the United States, but he must have large customers in all of the Pacific rim nations!"

"In the end we must realize that our lives are brief, very brief. To simply survive is an insufficient challenge. The real challenge of a human being is to make their life truly valuable. This, interestingly enough, is done from the inside, where all real value is fostered, and brought into a functional reality only as we give it away. So, to you who would get the most from this time, I say, listen well to your companions. Especially listen to the thoughts between the words. Listen for the heart and the spirit and gather these treasures for life!"

Jim applauded enthusiastically and wrote quickly in his journal. He noticed several others jotting notes in a journal, too and felt right at home. He thought about the truth of becoming like your five closest associates. Weinberg patted him on the shoulder. Jim reached across the table and wrapped his fingers around the ice water glass. It was cool and wet to the touch. Sweating, as Andy would say. As he drank deeply, the cold water seemed to invigorate his entire system. He felt totally alive.

Nina from Germany addressed the group next. She talked of her first exposure to the Safari Adventure Company as a young girl. Her father was an earlier member and ran the Company location in Berlin for many years. She talked about the business side of the Company and how the investments were doing extremely well. The Company was very wealthy and contributions continued to pour in. There were plans to expand and offer many new opportunities to share the ideas that had touched so many lives to people all over the world who would not or could not take the time for the safari.

Jim learned how the club was structured and how far reaching the influence of the group was. He was impressed at the very strict discipline and high degree of accountability that they applied to all they did. It was amplified by the fact that the overall impression was one of fun and adventure, not rules and regulations.

"Discipline," said Nina, "is not a prison wall, but instead it is a framework to assure freedom."

Finally the last man was introduced. Kipper simply called him Armstrong, and invited the muscular American to the microphone. The blond haired, blue eyed man in the baseball jacket walked confidently to the podium.

"What words could I add to these?" he wondered aloud thoughtfully. "To share this time with the brilliant Nina, my beloved Songh, and the legendary Kipper is an honor and privilege.

"Tomorrow you will begin a journey unlike any other you have ever taken. The mentoring process where you will each be assigned an experienced companion has been very effective and most enjoyable. I think you can sense that from the words shared by everyone tonight. We encourage you to have fun and be creative.

"However, I must warn you. Hear me well. You may have been lulled into a sense of playground amusement park mentality. This is not such a place. The African jungle, despite our roads and preparations, is still a very dangerous place. The jeeps each have a radio and a high powered shotgun, and each of you will be given a pistol. The particular area we are in is inhabited by lions, leopards, elephants, and several other extremely dangerous and unpredictable animals. You will be given some basic training to identify many of the plants and insects that can cause harm so remember your training and stick close to your guides for assistance and advice.

"There have been rumors of poachers in the area of the Nyika National Park. We have requested the local authorities to be vigilant in their efforts to rid the place of this menace. If encountered, these men would be extremely dangerous. They protect their turf like drug lords and are usually tied in to the local community by their relatives. They are tough to catch. Do not try to interfere or be a hero. If you encounter these types, steer clear and report in later. They will be avoiding you, to be sure."

After making several other the routine announcements, Armstrong relaxed a bit.

"I have to tell you that there has not been anything near a serious accident in 20 years. We go to great lengths to keep the safari safe.

"I also have to tell you that many years ago I was on

the safari that had the accident. One of the newcomers was constantly trying to take off into the bush. He wanted to fling his machete and hack into all these impossible places. His companion wore himself to a frazzle trying to control this person but to no avail. They realized they had lost track of the young man one day after lunch. The entire group searched for two days before we finally found his remains. He had been attacked by a lion and devoured. The clothing and pack were all that was left to identify the young man. It is indeed a very dangerous place to be foolish. But, a wonderful place to the wise. As the great prophet once said, He who has ears, let him listen!'"

After the speakers had concluded, the men and women of the Safari Adventure Company broke into ever changing groups. They busily renewed old friendships and made new ones. The "green peas" were back-slapped and encouraged to call themselves members now. The veterans did everything to make them feel at home.

As it grew late, Jim realized how very tired he was. He bid everyone good evening and climbed the stairs to the room. Jim took a quick shower. The hot water relieved his muscles and stress and felt so good. He toweled dry and slipped beneath the soft sheets.

He was in Africa. He was in this incredible place. Before he turned out the light he pulled his copy of "The Three Treasures" out of his bag, turned to the opening page and read:

The Three Treasures
London, England 1895
The Royal Safari Adventure Company

We, the members in good stead with the Royal Safari Adventure Company, do herewith set forth our great hope that you, the reader, will avail yourself of the wisdom contained on these pages. The principles here are time-tested and strong. You need know from the beginning that you will always be as unhappy as you are this otherwise fine day, unless you come to realize that happiness does not lie on the outerside of your life.

If you seek fulfillment in the 'things' of this reality, you are doomed to be ruled by circumstance, unforeseeable luck, and the whims of others who care not a whit for you or your lot. These will be your masters as you struggle to fill the void in your life with the stuff of materialism. For you see, dear voyager, you will never be truly happy until you gain the understanding that joy is to be found inside of you. There are certain joys, we call them treasures, that you may possess despite the winds of change that blow on us all. The Three Treasures herein will serve you well if you recall to measure and add to them every day. Neglect to care for them often, and you will go there one day to find them gone, sifted

away a little at a time like flour through a hole in the bottom of a miller's sack.

Gather these treasures, for they are there for everyone. Seek them and your life will be richer than any King who lies awake at night, sleepless despite his rooms filled with gold. Protect them, never let anyone trick you into trading them for the passing pleasures of this world, and they will comfort you in your golden years and put you at peace about the life beyond.

Jim closed the book and thought. It was true that he had relied on all the outside forces in the world to make him happy. Did everyone like him? Oh, how he had tried to fit in! How many times did his wife help him by insisting he change shirt and pants to get "the look?" Did he make enough money? Always searching for the feeling of having "arrived," and never getting there. He was not certain what the book meant by its treasures but he was open to the idea. Whatever he was doing now, it sure wasn't working!

He opened the journal Benjamin had given everyone on the plane.

"The thoughts, sights, sounds, and feelings you have here will be very important to your life. Don't let them escape!" he had warned. "Capture the memories in this journal in your words in this space in time."

Jim wondered what to write. "Dear Diary" came to

mind. He laughed at his own silliness. Though very tired he wrote his first thoughts:

> *"This is a once in a lifetime opportunity. There is something I must learn here. If I listen carefully and think through what I hear, I will find something just for me. I commit to listen to Weinberg and learn from him the lesson that he has to share. I am at a real crossroads in my life right now. I hope I can see clearly what the next step is for me while I am here."*

Jim turned out the light and took a deep breath. The bed felt like heaven and the pillow was just right. Sleep came at once.

THE LAKE OF STARS

Jim opened one eye and realized where he was after a brief moment of disorientation. Weinberg was already up and gone. Jim peered at his watch through sleepy eyes and realized it was almost noon! Splashing some water on his face he dressed quickly and headed downstairs.

Walking through the large doors of the dining hall, Jim was absorbed by a crowd of people noisily filing through a buffet of the most delicious looking food he had ever seen. Jim was absolutely ravenous and went straight to work deciding and choosing the first plate.

He fell in line with the others and stretched his arms high to wake the muscles that were still sore from his sleep-a-thon. He heard a voice and looked down to see a smiling face looking back up.

"This is some place, yes?" asked Tatsuro as he stepped in line behind Jim. It was the young Japanese man Jim had met the night before.

"Yeah, I can't believe I'm really here. I just woke up. How about you?"

"I, too, slept like a stone. As tall as you are, you must sleep like the log!" he said to the much taller

Jim. "It is not like me to be the most lazy one. I have never been in a plane so long! I think you call it "jet-legs?"

"Yes, that's it." said Jim, smiling at the funny mispronunciation.

After filling their plates with various fruits and rolls, Jim and Tatsuro grabbed the nearest table.

"I am to be in Group 12. How about you?" Tatsuro asked him.

"Hey, I'll be with you! I'm in Group 12, too!"

They both began to talk excitedly at the same time. Laughing, Jim invited Tatsuro to go first. He was a quality manager at an automobile manufacturer in Japan. He had twin girls at home, teenagers.

"My wife and I are having a difficult time with them." He said smiling. "Teenagers today are so different, so materialistic. They want to have everything the parent has. They do not understand that it took their parents years to gradually accumulate possessions and knowledge as well as privilege."

Jim nodded in agreement and told about the Nike's Claire just had to have that cost over $160.

Tatsuro countered with the painful price of American blue jeans.

"The villain is television and its relentless advertising," said Tatusro flatly. "My father say, television is awful and should be removed from the house, except if there is a big game on!"

They laughed their agreement and understood how

much they had in common. Their discussion was interrupted by the loud clanging of a bell. This brought the whole group to silence. Turning toward the noise, they saw their host, Arthur Kipper.

"At this time we must begin to ready ourselves for the journey. The vehicles will depart in one hour to Lake Malawi. Please be on time. You will have one hour to finish your meal and pack. You must report to the buses located just outside the main lodge. Now, before we undertake our journey, let us give thanks and ask for guidance with a prayer. Benjamin would you do the honors?"

Benjamin removed his bush hat and cleared his throat.

Prayer! Jim thought they only did that at football games and banquet invocations. He looked around slyly to see what others were doing. Most just sort of bowed their head so he did the same thing, still looking around with one eye.

"Dear God, we stand here before you today certain of two things," began Benjamin solemnly, "one, that we're not you, the one true and livin' God, and two, that we're not what we ought to be. We've made decisions we're not proud of and have failed at times to do the right thing. Let us be filled with the power that only comes from you to learn, grow, change, and become the kind of people you can use. Help us to build new and lasting friendships to strengthen us in the years that lie ahead. Protect each person here throughout the safari and throughout their journeys.

Bring everyone home safely. Thank you for your love, kindness, and grace. In Jesus' name, Amen."

Jim was not a religious person. He hadn't been to church in years and suspected most church goers were either right wing hypocrites or kooks. Was this some kind of psycho-babble cult? His suspicion meter went up immediately. He would watch carefully. No one would take advantage of him!

Quickly finishing their breakfast, Jim and Tatsuro parted long enough to go back to get their knapsacks and gear for the trip. Within moments Jim was back in front of the main lodge, searching for his bus. Weinberg was already on board when he arrived.

"Hullo, Sleepyhead," he said, good naturedly. "Are you rested?"

"Yes, Sir, I am. I feel great," said Jim taking the seat he had been saving for him. They chatted easily. Andy soon joined them.

"Are you ready for the trip, Andy?" asked Jim, happy to see his buddy.

"I am fed and watered and ready to go!" Andy called back as he plopped down on the seat next to Weinberg. "Hey, Tatsuro, how are those jet legs?"

Tatsuro waved and joined them. "Legs are good!" he said, patting his knees and smiling.

Andy had been the one to explain jet lag to Tatsuro who had found the pun to be hilarious. Andy had such a good funny bone he could even explain jokes in other cultures!

Benjamin and the others soon arrived. The bus pulled out and headed past Lake Malombe and down the valley to the southern end of the third largest lake in Africa, Lake Malawi.

The driver popped in an audio cassette of some local singing group that was absolutely magical. The melodic rhythm had everyone tapping their feet to the bouncing bass line and trying to sing along with the choruses. Though they did not understand a word of the language, the energy of the group was definitely on key!

"Dr. Livingstone, the Scottish missionary, did a lot of work in Lake Malawi. He was the first European to set eyes on this lake back in 1859. It is the third largest lake in Africa. Livingstone loved it so much he called it the Lake of Stars. It is a beautiful blue spot on the planet with white sandy beaches and all kinds of wildlife, especially birds." said Weinberg. He was a bit of a history buff and seemed to know all kinds of amazing facts about lots of places. They all listened as he continued.

"Under the surface is another universe. There are actually more species of fish here than in any other fresh water lake in the world. There are private lakeside cottages at the site where we are headed. They are all made from native materials and quite charming. During our three days there we will be able to choose from many activities designed to view and experience this wonderful place so few have ever seen."

Benjamin added, "Weinberg is right. There are catamaran cruises to the islands and fishin' villages. There is a scuba diving school, or you can snorkel. Either way is excellent for viewin' all the beautiful flippers."

"That's for me!" said Andy, puffing his cheeks, pretending to hold his breath and swim to the laughter of the happy group.

Time melted into distance, and soon the bus had arrived in paradise. Jim put his things in his cabin and took a brief walk down by the lake. It was warm and inviting. He pulled his new old favorite hat off and looked at the activity. There were already others there swimming, windsurfing and sailing small, one man sailboats near the lodge. Dinner would be served soon on the verandah overlooking the lake up at the main area. He returned to the cabin to wash up and change clothes before joining the others.

The evening became the night as the group continued their good natured fun and revelry. Jim and Andy settled on the wide verandah and talked as the staff lit large torches around the entire area. The firelight lent its ancient comfort and magic to the cool evening air. Jim breathed deeply of the forest and lake.

A large wooden backgammon game was on the table nearby and Andy pulled it over and set up the pieces. Jim leaned over the board and smiled, relearning an old game he used to play for hours with Tracey when they were young and broke.

It was so relaxing and peaceful here, Jim decided

to let himself forget about the problems that seemed so confusing at home. Just for now, he thought, I am going to enjoy not worrying. Tomorrow there would be enough to do.

"Red or black?" asked Andy.

"Red, I am always red!" Jim smiled as he pulled the rattan chair up to the board.

THE FIRST TREASURE

The next morning Jim was up early. The sun had just started to embrace the camp with its warmth. He sat on the steps outside the cabin and opened "The Three Treasures." They had been encouraged to read the First Treasure again in preparation for the morning session. Benjamin would lead the class, and Jim wanted to be ready. The sessions with Benjamin were rare and full of ideas.

THE TREASURE OF THE MIND

And be not conformed to this world; but be ye transformed by the renewing of your mind, that you may prove what is that good, and acceptable, and perfect will of God. Romans 12:2.

Your mind is the starting point of any significant success you will ever know. If it is muddled, cloudy, and fraught with the baggage of lies and negativity from your past, you are doomed to live inside a blueprint of a circle of unhappiness, always expecting the worst and being unsurprised at its predictable arrival. Like an ox at the threshing wheel, you will continue to walk the same sad path over and over without knowing any better.

You need to understand right now it is not entirely your fault that you are here at this particular point on the map of life. You have undoubtedly been helped to arrive here by misguided and unwitting accomplices. It is, however, imperative that you realize clearly that you need not remain.

Each fall, as the days begin to grow short, the robin will answer the call of the Creator to take wing and head south. When the winter begins to subside, he will turn north again and grace the northern latitudes with his announcement of springtime. When the fall comes, he will do it all over again. He has no choice. He is a physical machine of God's nature. You are not a robin!

You can totally change your life forever starting today, and the only reason it will stay the same is if YOU CHOOSE NOT TO CHANGE!

You can only choose what you can see, and here is the land of the mind. A man cannot choose to depart for a destination if he knows not of the place. To become a better thinker, you must become a serious student. Reading of books is the single most significant investment you will ever make to life-changing.

The First Treasure

Within the pages of a book one may know firsthand the struggle of another person's lifetime and the answers they have found. Real answers paid for with a thousand sleepless nights and incredible investments of time and effort boiled down to a few pages. The sights, sounds, and emotions of battles, adventures, and far away lands for the tiny investment of a few hours in a chair by a lamp. If you do not read, you are little better off than the savage who cannot read!

Conversation is the next tool of the wealthy mind. Not the coarse, vulgar, and idle chatter of the dim-witted. Instead, we urge you to seek opportunity to meet and learn from great philosophers. They are everywhere. People of experience and substance. Attend plays, lectures, and be frequent at the clubs and establishments, such as will attract someone who can change your life. By this we mean a mentor. The people who have grown to such great heights in their insides will be generous to give it away. Not to fools who spill the precious knowledge on the way out the door, but to eager seekers who demonstrate their sincere desire to grow.

One hour spent in the company of such a one will be more beneficial than any year in a university! Be patient in this search and know that the fit between two people will happen, seemingly quite by accident, and will be better seen in hindsight as to the ease with which this great event took place.

WARNING! The greatest hazard to possessing this treasure is the temptation to fill your treasure chest with worthless things. The world is changing rapidly around us and the voluminous wagons full of information are everywhere assaulting each of us. We must learn to separate the trash from the treasure and not waste valuable mental resource and time on the things that not only do not help, but actually pull us down the opposite path.

There is a lot of truth in this idea, thought Jim. He had not read a book in a long time. In fact, if he were honest with himself, most of the information he got was probably trash. Commercials, advertisements, and useless conversations about meaningless topics at the office. There were precious few quality conversations with his children. Tracey and he used to talk a lot about dreams and feelings, but now their communication was limited to mostly managing their commitments and money. As he closed "The Three Treasures," he decided to find and read a good book. Maybe Benjamin could recommend one.

Jim breathed in deeply the aroma of the trees that surrounded the camp. Passing a cabin, he smiled at a lady that joined him along the path to the little, open air amphitheater where Benjamin would give the workshop. They chatted easily along the dirt road lined with its split pine rail fence.

He could not honestly remember feeling this good since he was a child going to the lake with his uncle and aunt. His health and energy were fantastic. Andy was already there and waved Jim over to a seat next to him on the back row. Andy liked to sit in the back row and whisper little remarks and puns that kept Jim and whoever else was around laughing, including the instructors. Everyone liked Andy.

They had become fast friends and shared some powerful insights with one another around the large wooden tables in the lodge by the fireplace. Their backgrounds were completely different. Jim was Mr. Corporate America with the formal education. Andy was an ex rock and roll musician. He bragged that he attended the College of Musical Knowledge and the School of Hard Knocks. Like two Titanic passengers who had been traveling in different classes in the ship, one in luxury, one in steerage, their background mattered little. They were now both hitting the icy water together and had everything in common!

Benjamin stood and greeted the group. Standing at the front of the amphitheater with the bronze sunlight streaking across the gentle waves of the lake behind him, he looked as if he were an ancient philosopher plucked from another time. He had added to his familiar khaki and plaid outfit an Australian bush hat and looked like a movie poster. Jim captured

The Safari Adventure Company

the scene in his mind and wished he had a camera.

"Good morning campers!" Benjamin began, as usual, with his gusto and smile. He did not usually teach classes, but instead focused on counseling and administrative matters. It was good to see him here this morning, and the group was eager to spend the time with him.

"I promised all of you that we would be sharin' some information that you could use not only here but all the rest of your days. Of all the wonderful things I have learned since associatin' with the Safari Adventure Company, one of the most incredible has been learnin' to set and achieve goals.

"Now most people roll their eyes when I talk about goal settin' cause they've heard it all their lives. Not many actually write their goals down and what they call their goals are no more that a wish list. I like to say that sayin I wish' means it's just a dream without energy behind it. Somethin' you want but are not willing' to do what it takes to make it happen.

"I didn't harness the power of goal settin' until I learned a simple way to actually do it. This here is what I will share with you this morning.

"Now when I say "get it," I want you to say "got it" and I will say "good!" Let's try that now."

"Get it?" he said leaning forward to bait their response.

"Got it!" shouted the group enthusiastically.

"Good!" said Benjamin with a big smile.

"Step one is to take a blank sheet of paper and

write a master dream list. On this list try to get at least 50 items. Things you would like to do, places to visit, possessions, experiences you want to have, skills you want to learn, and achievements that are important to you. Where do you want to be, what do you want to accomplish in the next 10 years?

The important thing here is to get the juices flown' and go for quantity. Just a word or two will be enough. You don't have to write a paragraph about everythin'. Just get it out there on paper. I will give you about 15 minutes to make a first list."

"Get it?"

"Got it!" They shouted, smiles everywhere.

"Good! Let's go."

Jim popped out a few things he wanted to buy. Golf clubs and small things. Then he stopped. He had never sat down and thought about where he wanted to be in ten years. His whole life had been dictated by the "track" at the company. He sat in embarrassed silence as the scratching sound of pencil and paper captured dreams all around him.

Andy poked him and pointed to the most recent item he had written.

"What is the Air Aces?" asked Jim.

"They take you up in a fighter plane and you get to actually fly the plane, with an instructor of course, and have dogfights and all kinds of cool stuff!" he said excitedly. "I have always wanted to do that."

Jim nodded and smiled. Andy did not lack imagination.

Benjamin surveyed the group and asked no one in particular, "What would you like your life to look like on a daily basis? What activities, what kind of work, what kind of life do you want? If you don't plan it for yourself, you will always be a part of someone else's plan."

Jim added some vacation spots and other small items, but he was agitated by the idea that he could not come up with a major life goal or dream. He was unemployed and uprooted from his field. What would he do when the Safari was over? Benjamin's voice interrupted. Had fifteen minutes gone by so quickly?

"The next step is to place a number next to each goal. A number 1, 3, 5, or 10, will indicate if this is a goal you intend to reach in one year, three and so on. Let's do that now. If you find you have a lot of 1's and 3's and no 5's and 10's, it may be that you are short sighted and not willing' to face the big picture. If, on the other hand you have all 5's and 10's, you may be puttin' everythin' off to some far away future and not takin' action."

Jim looked down at his 1's and 3's and frowned.

Benjamin pressed on. "Then I want you to take the top four goals for each time frame, your top 1's, top 3's and so on and transfer them to a separate page. Let's start with our top one year goals. The best way to select them is to ask, If I could only achieve one of these, which would I like for it to be? Then one more until you have your four."

"Then I want you to write a few sentences about

The First Treasure

each goal. Describe it in detail. Also, you should add the reasons why you want to achieve this goal. The reasons why are the power behind the action you will need to take to get where you want to go. Frankly, if you lack reasons why, you do not have a goal at all and you will never do the necessary work to make it a reality."

"Get it?"

"Got it!"

"Good!"

The group went back to work with excitement now. Jim observed the faces. Some were smiling; some had furrowed brows and serious looks. Jim wrote the instructions down, but did not do the exercise. He looked over at Andy's list. He was working on an income goal for his sales for the rest of the year. His reasons why were numerous and powerful. To provide things for his wife and daughters, and the self esteem that it would bring, would be strong motivators when the days seemed tough and he felt like quitting.

Benjamin's voice called him back to the exercise.

"The next step is to write a game plan for each goal. What actions do you intend to take, what books can you read, what classes can you take, who can you talk to or take out to lunch and interview, what kind of person must you become in order to earn the right to accomplish this dream? Plan it and lay it out in little steps. Remember, you eat an elephant one bite at a time!"

Andy made a sound like the trumpet of an elephant, and everyone laughed loudly.

"Then, you must track your progress on a regular basis. Set up a chart to review your numbers—how many pages read, how many miles run—whatever you are accomplishin'. The devil's in the little numbers. Here is why.

Imagine we're all boardin' a beautiful sailin' ship that is sittin' in New York Harbor bound for London. Three days out, the ship is forty feet off course. Now that is a rather small adjustment, isn't it? But, do you know, that if the captain never watches these little numbers and therefore never makes that slight adjustment, by the time he gets across the sea he can be a thousand miles away from where he ever intended to go?

I see so many people who have a goal, and even think up a plan to get there, but the little things in life push them off course. Then one day they are 30, the next mornin' they are 40, or 50 and their lives end up a thousand miles away from where they thought they were goin'."

Benjamin's voice seemed to break as he looked away wistfully across the lake behind him and then back to the eyes of the group.

"Don't let that happen to you! Set your goals. Believe in yourself and your right to live your dreams. Keep workin on your plan to make it happen."

"Finally, I want to share a magic secret that will give you incredible power in this quest. Every day, do somethin', no matter how small, toward accomplishin' your major goal. The one goal, that if you accomplish it, will have the most significant impact on all the others. Read a few pages in that book. Pick up the phone and order a brochure on that class you have been meanin' to take. Schedule a lunch with someone who is already successful at what you want to become. You take these simple steps and you will truly see, the greatest adventure is the rest of your life!

"Get it?"

"Got it!"

"Good!"

The next afternoon was a day off from the training. Most spent the day exploring the fascinating lake area. Jim had asked to meet Benjamin in the library. Benjamin reserved one of the little study cubicles in the back so he could talk with Jim without disturbing any others.

Benjamin said openly, "You said you wanted to see me, Jim. What's on your mind?"

"First, I just want to thank you for inviting me here. I've already had a tremendous time." said Jim.

He listened to himself excitedly describe his experience at the camp in that strange way you can be talking and yet hearing yourself. He knew he sounded a bit like a kid, but who better should he express his joy about the camp than to Benjamin?

The two men talked for half an hour about the Safari Adventure Company and the upcoming trip. Then there was a moment of silence, the awkward kind where both people realize they were not listening but thinking of something else and didn't know quite what to say next, or who should say it.

"Benjamin," began Jim in a calmer tone, "I had a real problem with the goal setting workshop yesterday morning."

"What was your concern, Jim? Did you disagree with the concepts?" said Benjamin.

"No, the concepts were very sound to me. I used to do a lot of strategic planning on my job. Your ideas were great," said Jim.

"Then, what was troublin' you?" Benjamin asked again.

Jim sensed the same concern and clarity Benjamin had shown the day he interviewed with him the first time he entered the Safari American Headquarters. He knew it was safe, even wise, to be open with his friend.

"The problem was not with the workshop. The problem was with me! I couldn't set any real goals. I couldn't see any direction for my life. I have lost my job. I have been discredited falsely. My kids are ignoring me and my wife has practically disowned me!" Jim looked up at Benjamin. The pain in his eyes was easy to see.

"I told the truth. I took the high road. It kicked me in the teeth. Where is Winston Churchill now?" Jim said in a half joking tone. It was hard to describe how confusing it was to be so happy with the safari and so miserable inside.

"Simple does not always mean easy, Jim. You did the right thing at your work. You know you did. I'm sure it's been hard, but you need to remember that this jam you're in is only temporary," Benjamin started.

"I guess I will get another job somewhere and I know I did the right thing, but why can't I set new goals?" I just went blank when we did the master list. What's going to happen to me after this fantasy trip is over?" Jim interjected, his anger poorly disguised. He was beginning to honestly feel the feelings that were being put off by all the activity and hope of the trip.

Benjamin continued with a caring smile, "Jim, it is going to be very difficult for you to see the big picture of your future until some of the clutter is cleared from today. Anyone undergoin' such a significant emotional event, like you are, would have an awful lot on their plate to deal with. Do you really want my advice on this, or do you just want to talk it out?"

"I already have a great talk it out' partner in Andy. We have had some great conversations. I would like some advice. Have you got any how to's?" Jim asked hopefully with a little smile.

"Okay, here goes," said Benjamin, drawing a deep breath. "You need to know that time is needed for you to get clarity. You have undergone a real crisis in your life and it is not over. There are two obstacles compoundin' your situation.

"The first one is external. It has to do with your family, your job and your social situation. You have always taken these for granted. They were just a part of the landscape of your life. You didn't have to do much to maintain them. Now they are cavin' in on you because you don't have the crutch of your job to brace them up.

"Your desire to put your world back together again is extremely stressful because it's practically impossible. You cannot go back into the past, though it's natural to long for a time when things were predictable, even if they had their own pain and unfulfillment. We often tend to forget the truth about the past when the present begins to challenge us. You must accept the fact that your external world must be reconstructed, and it is goin' to take time.

"The second obstacle is the greater. That obstacle is you," Benjamin stated bluntly and nodded in Jim's direction.

"What do you mean, me?" Jim shot back defensively.

"You are in danger of withdrawin' into a pity-pot. Feelin' sorry for yourself and blamin' your situation on others," said the big Australian leaning back in his chair.

"Hey! I didn't cause the problem at work. I didn't alienate my wife and kids. If anyone has a right to feel sorry for himself, it's me!" Jim protested.

"I will be the first to agree that you are in an unfortunate situation. You must understand clearly that the

The First Treasure

road to happiness is not goin' to be found by tryin' to fix other people. Blamin' is a waste of time. If you want to get back in the game, you must take responsibility for your own life. You will be the one who stands up and takes the steps to rebuild your world. You must accept that things are the way they are, and now you must fearlessly operate in that reality."

Jim started to speak, but Benjamin lifted a finger for Jim to wait for him to finish.

"We feel happiest to the degree in which we feel in control of our own lives. You must now get it straight that you are the captain of your own destiny. The courage, strength, and faith to go from this crossroads in your life to a place of peace and contentment will be found in your understandin' this idea," Benjamin declared.

"But, I don't even know which way to go," Jim said again, throwing up his hands sadly.

"Time, Jim. Give it a little time. I know this sounds too simple but for now, if you will focus on the inside person, the only thing you can control, you, your thoughts, your attitudes, your mind, very soon the new horizon will appear. You will see clearly your direction. The path, and the power to reach it, will come afterwards," declared Benjamin confidently, patting Jim on the shoulder.

"What do I do in the meantime?" asked Jim weakly.

Benjamin smiled and said, "It's just a mean time!"

"Oh, great." Jim's lanky frame slumped down in

the chair.

Benjamin added, "A good place to start is "The Three Treasures." Have you read the book?"

"Yes, I have been challenged to start to read again and learn a little, you know, improve my mind," said Jim. "All that religious stuff seems unnecessary, though.

"Do the verses bother you, Jim?" asked Benjamin.

"Not anymore," Jim responded, realizing Benjamin often answered his questions with a question, but not really sure how to turn it around without saying so.

"They are actually very thought provoking. But, I'm not a very religious person Benjamin, are you?"

"What do you mean by a religious person?"

"I guess I mean someone who thinks he is better than everyone else because he is such a "holy roller" and goes around criticizing everyone else for having fun." Jim realized as soon as he said it what a cliché this was.

"Is that what you see when you look at me?" Benjamin asked in a non-threatening way.

"Gosh, no, Benjamin! I mean, hey, you know, you're all right. You don't go around telling everyone how to live. Everyone admires you. Where do you stand on religion?"

"Listen mate, I have a great regard for the spiritual, but not much of what passes for religion."

"How about the Bible then? I will agree it's got some good stuff in it, but do you really believe it's true? he said.

The First Treasure

"Absolutely," nodded Benjamin. "That is exactly what I believe."

Benjamin walked to a book on the middle shelf and opened it. He began to show Jim how the Bible was created by dozens of writers who wrote independently of each other over hundreds of years without any contradiction. He showed him how the monks had preserved the writings for centuries. The pains they took to preserve the accuracy of these sacred hand written manuscripts was incredible.

He explained how they would count every vowel and consonant forward and backward. They totaled the words and letters and found the middle word and middle letter of each chapter and each book. Erroneous copies were destroyed. Meticulously they labored in love, their lives devoted, and sometimes sacrificed, to their legacy.

Jim was impressed with this big, rough, safari trainer. Not only was he very knowledgeable, you could tell he had a strong faith in what he believed. Jim realized he personally believed in very little of what you might call, absolute truth. Everything in his world was relative. Even the decision to expose the wrong doing at the company was more a matter of his unwillingness to live with the lie than his sense of right and wrong.

"If you don't stand for something, you will fall for anything!" he had heard someone say. It had stuck in Jim's head, and he saw the truth of that here. Benjamin believed something. Although Jim didn't believe the things Benjamin did, he could only sit in admiration at his new friend's enthusiasm and love for the Bible and his obvious scholarship.

"I tried to read the Bible once," said Jim remembering his days in a college philosophy class. "It was boring and hard to read, with all the thee and thous and weird names. I just gave up."

Benjamin looked Jim squarely in the eye and said, "Mate, you will never realize what you have been missin' until you read the Bible for yourself as an adult. The history and all this are mere pips on the radar screen compared to the power of what you will find there for your everyday walk.

That's what "The Three Treasures" is all about at the heart of the matter. Look, Jim, no matter who is in the White House, where you live, or what is goin' on in your life, you can have these Three Treasures in abundance to bring you joy and value. They don't depend on external circumstances. Nothin' in life worth havin' is external. Only the inner things really matter! That is real life, Jimmy boy!

You don't start anythin' at the finish line. You start at the beginnin'. You're goin' through a awfully tough time, Jim. You must have faith in yourself and believe you will win," Benjamin encouraged.

"But I have no faith; I have no belief," said Jim mournfully.

Benjamin became serious in his tone, still smil-

The First Treasure

ing he said, "Here, then, start by believin' in belief and havin' faith that there is faith. If you reach for these ideas, you will find what you are lookin' for, guaranteed!"

Benjamin slapped him on the back and smiled broadly. Jim grinned like he'd won a prize. Without a word there appeared that special moment when faith made that unbelievable leap from the heart of one person to another. Suddenly, Jim was aware of a warm feeling of contented happiness. He had only scratched the surface of what Benjamin had shared, but his strength to believe a new truth for the first time depended not on him but on the truth itself. It was borne on the spirit of its own power, set aloft by the certainty of Benjamin's knowing.

After bidding Benjamin good night in the library, Jim walked alone down by the amphitheater. The burning torches across the lake made a tiny golden ballet of light in the dark rippling water.

Jim lay back on the benches and looked up at the infinite number of stars in the cloudless African sky. The power of the created universe swept over him and begged for his attention. There he opened his heart to the possibility of a happiness that did not depend on Tracey, money, or any of the other things he had hoped would tell him he was good enough. It made absolute sense. Yes, it was possible. It felt that right.

Everyone was asleep when Jim slipped quietly into the cabin and tiptoed past Andy to his own bunk. He lay down in his clothes to rest for just a moment and sleep came quickly.

He dreamed again of the tiger. It was so vivid. The shocking orange and black colors rolled silently across the muscular frame of the ferocious killer. Yet this time Jim was not afraid. He heard the parrot's wings and saw the whole thing happen both in slow motion and in a fraction of a second.

This time there was someone else right beside him. They were moving toward the tiger. He did not recognize the older man who protected him but he felt safe because of his presence. The jungle turned into his living room at home in that strange way dreams do. The rest was lost.

Standing in line the next morning to use the pay phone Jim began to get nervous. This would not be an easy call. Tomorrow they would head into the bush and there would not be another opportunity to call until the end of the safari.

The man in front of him said his good-byes and hung up the phone. He nodded to Jim as he passed. The phone felt warm from all the hand-holding as Jim gave his credit card information to the operator. His heart rate went up double as the distant yet familiar ring of his home phone came to his ear. His daughter Claire said hello.

"Hi, Claire," called out Jim hopefully.

The First Treasure

"Daddy, is that you?" she asked.

"Yes, it's me," he laughed and started to tell her about the upcoming Safari.

"I'll get mom," she said and dropped the phone to the table without waiting to hear his reply. Her rejection stung like the harsh sound of the phone falling. All he could do was shake his head silently and try not to get mad.

After a few moments, he heard the sound of voices down the hall talking argumentatively. Footsteps came closer and gave way to the sound of the phone being retrieved, (from the floor?) Tracey's voice asked, "What is it?"

"Hi, Honey," Jim tried to begin positively.

"Don't you hi honey me, Jim. What do you want?

"We are breaking camp here in the morning and will be in the bush for the next ten days. I will not be able to call until then and I thought you would want to know."

Tracey cut him off. "Is there anything else? I am very busy," said Tracey flatly.

"Tracey, you knew I was going to do this from the start. When I signed up, you said you didn't care what I did and would be glad I was out of the house for a..."

"Listen and listen good, Jim," Tracey interrupted, "I have had it with you and this whole thing. Our friends think you are nuts and the people from the plant keep calling to ask questions. I am tired of all this. But, most of all I am tired of you!"

"I've changed since coming here. It has really done me so much good, you'll see," Jim pleaded as he looked around to see if anyone could hear him shame himself.

"I have had time to think, too, since you have been there. I think we would be better off apart and the kids do, too," she continued coldly.

"Aww, Tracey come on, the kids? Calm down and let me explain what is going on," he said.

"Did you read the letter? That explains what's going on. I am not seeing anyone else. (Jim's mind went reeling at that. He hadn't imagined his wife would even think of being unfaithful.) I just feel like we'd be better off apart," she declared.

"Come on, let's just talk. The time I am here will help you think more clearly," Jim tried.

"I am thinking clearly—more clearly than ever before. Please don't try to come home now either. We would just fight. Let me take this time to think, Jim. I just need some time to think." At the last few words her voice broke and Jim could hear her trying to hide a crying sound with her hand over her mouth.

"Oh, Tracey," Jim started to speak but the phone went dead.

Jim realized she had hung up on him. Hurt, angry, and frustrated, he slammed the pay phone down on the hook and growled angrily, teeth clenched. Turning around he realized there was a lady in a light blue jogging suit waiting to use the phone. They smiled politely at one another and looked away quickly. She stepped past him and up to the phone.

Jim heard her say, "Hi, Honey!" to the person on the other end. "Oh, I miss you too! You are just going to love this place! We have got to do this together next time!"

Her happy words stung Jim's heart. He could feel the energy draining and the bitter anger burning in his neck. He clenched his fists as he walked away to nowhere.

He did not notice Andy until he put his hand on Jim's shoulder. Jim whirled around, revealing his distress.

"Hey, buddy!" Andy shook his friend. "What did you do, eat a lizard?" he said looking at Jim's painful face.

"Oh, hi, Andy, how are you?" Jim asked automatically.

"Better than you, it looks," said Andy, changing gears instantly. He could see this was no time for comedy. "What's going on?"

"Aww, I just tried to talk to Tracey and she just really tore into me."

Andy put his arm around Jim and shook him roughly as he laughed. "Come on, let's get a cup of coffee and you can tell me all about it." The two men turned and headed back up across the camp to the lodge.

WILDERNESS

"Hold on a minute!" shouted a familiar voice. Andy ran up to the group out of breath.

"I just wanted to say good luck and have a tremendous time. I will be taking another route with Benjamin and his group. We will meet up again at the half way station," Andy said excitedly as the two men shook hands warmly.

"Good luck to you, my friend. I hope you have the adventure of a lifetime," said Jim.

" Oh, Weinberg, don't let Jim play with any African tigers," Andy warned, teasing Jim about the dream he had shared.

"There are no tigers in Africa," said Weinberg matter-of-factly to Jim.

"I know that," said Jim, embarrassed, "he's just kidding."

Andy turned and trotted back to his group calling, "Hey! Benjamin! I got dibs on the shotgun seat!"

Jim turned to continue listening to the instructions of the guide. Gabriel was a native African in his mid 30s, tall and muscular with a serious face. He wore tan shorts and a sleeveless bush shirt that amplified his powerful build. Jim worried that the young guide may lack experience.

"Do not be fooled by the warm humid weather here at the bottom of this valley," warned Gabriel. " We are going to climb steadily the next two days through the highlands of the Nyika National Forest. The elevation here at the lake is 470 meters. We are going to go to all the way to 2300 meters. The weather can get very cool and unpredictable. Take the proper clothing. We will be entering a vast forest. "Nyika" means "wilderness." You will soon know why."

Jim patted his bag, remembering his thicker bush coat, and made a mental inventory of all he had thought to bring.

"This is Stephen," announced Gabriel as he gestured toward the even younger man standing just a little behind him. Stephen was very dark complected and wore a moonbeam smile and a golden earring. His red bandana and Houston Rockets t-shirt made him look as if he had walked right off the streets of any American city.

"Hello, good to meet you all," he said with a sterling British accent as he stepped up confidently toward the group.

"So, you are a fan of the Rockets?" Jim asked Stephen.

"A what of the who?" Stephen replied with a quizzical expression.

"Never mind," said Jim.

Jim looked around at the others. There was the smiling Tatsuro with an older, but vibrant and excited Japanese man. The wiry, snowy haired man wore atheltic spectacles with a sports band. They were both clad in identical running suits that were obviously expensive and very sharp.

"This is my uncle, Ishido," said Tatsuro proudly. " He is a long time member of the Safari and my companion."

"Hello! I have heard a good deal about your work in Japan with young people. I am so glad to finally meet you," said Weinberg, bowing to the Japanese man.

Ishido bowed slightly in return and smiled vigorously at the group, revealing a mouthful of pearly white teeth.

"As they say in America, 'Let the good times roll!'" Ishido said as the others laughed.

"He loves American rhythm and blues," said Tatsuro laughing along.

"B.B. King is my man!"

Still chuckling, Weinberg introduced a short happy woman named Rosa. Dressed in a bright yellow blouse and khaki slacks, she looked like a vacationing tourist. Her makeup and hair were perfect. She said hello to each member of the group and shook their hands one at a time. Rosa was obviously what you would call a, "people-person!"

"Jim, it is so very nice to meet you!" she said.

"Weinberg has told me about you. You know, he is quite impressed with you. You must be someone special!"

Jim blushed and shook her hand gratefully. Her soft flowing South American accent were perfect companions for her graceful style.

"Now, where is my new little spark plug?" Rosa asked as she stood on her tiptoes and tried to survey the camp.

"Oh, there she is."

Rosa pointed in the direction of a scuffle. There was a man trying to help a young lady carry her pack, and she was having none of it. As they drew closer, Jim could hear her arguing and protesting. Finally, she jerked the pack from his arms and broke it free. The pack flew through the air and landed at Rosa's feet, barely missing a ducking Weinberg.

The girl darted into the middle of the group, retrieved the pack, stood and pulled a white designer baseball cap off her light brown, pony tailed hair.

"Karin!" said Rosa with great concern, "are you all right?"

"You bet, I just had to tell that sailor to shove off!" said the defiant Karin.

Jim rolled his eyes and turned away. There was something about the cocky girl that Jim could not tolerate. He made a mental note to have nothing to do with this irritating, in-your-face, pest.

Weinberg patted Jim on the shoulder. Jim had not attempted to conceal his agitation.

"We all go along through this life at our own speed," he said patiently. "Perhaps there is a reason she is in our group—something she has to teach you."

The Wilderness

Jim looked at his mentor in astonishment. That, he thought, was the dumbest thing Weinberg had said since he met him!

"I have been many times into this forest," Gabriel addressed the other seven members of the group. This part of Africa has not been inhabited by anyone for over a thousand years. Only the mysterious ruins of ancient ancestors hint at a time of settling long ago. There are only a few tiny villages there. You must be alert at all times."

Jim remembered the videos and lecture classes they had held both in America before departing and at the lake the last two days. The programs had been very well done, and he had gained a great deal of confidence in what he had learned about the dangers and benefits of the plants and habitat in the jungle.

"Each of you, with your companion, will have one of the four land rovers as your base. It is equipped with all you will need for our journey," explained Gabriel. "Go now, and check your supplies and ready yourself for departure."

Jim was more than ready to hit the road. "Weinberg, which vehicle is ours?" he asked anxiously.

"Just over there." Weinberg nodded toward their jeep.

Jim led the way and quickly began checking through their loaded supplies. Weinberg joined him and in no time they were seated and ready for the go ahead.

All around, the bustle of activity was being repeated by the other groups of eight. Finally, a singing call went out in a local tribal tongue from one guide to another.

As if on cue, the sound of the birds, chimpanzees and the commotion of the cranking engines rose a decibel as if a crowd were cheering a sporting event from the grandstand. Jim bristled with excitement and gripped the handle at the open door of the jeep tightly with both hands.

With Weinberg at the wheel, they fell in line behind the other three land rovers in their assembly led by Gabriel and Stephen. As they drove to the east, the smooth tar road gave way to gravel.

They passed banana and rubber plantations on their way up and out of the valley. The expansive Miombo Woodlands opened up and swallowed the jeeps. The trees, thick on each side of the man made road, reached up to brush the translucent sky, creating the effect of high walls about them. Because the road was still wide at this point, there was a large expanse of clear, blue sky to be seen overhead. Birds circled and flew from one outcrop of giant hardwood trees to the other.

The trees began to meet together overhead as the road narrowed upon their exit from the encampment. It seemed to Jim that early morning soon became late afternoon since the trees blocked out so much of the bright sunlight. Refocusing for the filtered light, he could now see how matted and tangled the undergrowth was around each of the trees. So many large roots intertwining among an endless variety of plant shapes.

Jim looked up high. The chatter of chimpanzees that he had continually heard during his stay at the lake now had faces. Swinging throughout the maze of branches were dozens of all kinds and sizes of chimps and other smaller monkeys. Their shining eyes were taking in the group's movement down the road with avid interest.

"So, Jim, what do you think now?" asked Weinberg with a little wink and a smile.

Jim smiled back, and took a deep breath. This was it. Here was the challenge to face the fears he had always felt, but never spoke. The grandiose scenery, the wide never-ending expanses he'd seen here in Africa, the powerful water flow he heard in the distance, and the sound of nature buzzing throughout this forest had transported him to another level.

He smiled to himself and took an even deeper breath, slowly exhaling as he slid down a bit in the in the seat. Tilting his hat to block out the bright sunlight, he was the man on the front of the brochure!

After they had been driving over an hour and a half, Stephen half-stood in the lead jeep, waved, then called out to the others following to pull over to the side of the now dirt road. On Gabriel's orders they all got out of their jeeps, took a stretch, and prepared a quick lunch.

It was clear that Gabriel, though young, was an absolute expert. Stephen and he worked as a seamless team. They were not, however, robotic and stiff. They, too, were having fun! Joking with the group, they made a rapid, but easy effort to get to know each one of the people in the team.

Jim thought how wonderful it must be to love your work!

"We are well on our way to get to our arranged campsite by early evening. Our pace is just right," announced Gabriel smiling. At that they all climbed into their vehicles and continued up the sloping road.

Jim had switched seats with Weinberg. The afternoon lay before him in the shape of a winding dirt road. He steered the jeep carefully as Weinberg kept him amused with stories of other safaris and tidbits of his family life.

His father had been an investment banker in Austria and his mother was an Englishwoman. She was a personal assistant for the president of a British bank doing business in eastern Europe. They had met at a business meeting where his father could not keep his eyes off the attractive prim and proper girl.

Although his father was Jewish and his mother was Catholic, they had fallen in love and moved to Austria. They were promptly tossed out of each other's church and synagogue for marrying outside the faith so they started attending a non-denominational Bible church.

"I grew up celebrating every holiday on the planet, from Passover to Christmas!" kidded Weinberg.

Time flew as the two men talked and laughed together and pointed out the interesting sights.

As the shadows grew longer, the little caravan pulled around a wide, slow bend. They all pulled their jeeps to the side of the road and sat and stared. No one spoke. Jim's mouth dropped open in astonishment as he sucked in a breath at the spectacle that lay before them.

Here was the highest point for miles around. With the sun at their backs, the layers of the forest had cleared to give way to a glorious sunset sweeping across the canyon and rolling mountains beyond.

Jim had never experienced such a vastness of natural beauty, unobstructed and devoid of man's touch. It was so precious and pure. He felt as if he were a child seeing the sunset for the first time. Even Karin was silent.

Everyone felt their own quiet strength drawn from the dignity and power of the mighty natural wonder. Jim looked at each of them and caught himself wondering about their feelings. It felt strange to care about the others.

As for himself, he couldn't help but think about how many sunsets like this he had missed, hunched over a computer or slugging it out in traffic trying to get home from the office.

He realized Weinberg, Stephen, and Tatsuro were beginning to set up the camp. The sounds of the more experienced campers unloading the gear brought him and the other "green peas" back to the task. They all began excitedly lending a hand with a renewed vigor. What a camp site!

Before long, their camp was established, the fires were started for cooking the meal, and each one could take a moment to have time to themselves either in their tents or by wandering the plateau they had overtaken for the night.

Rosa and Karin were taking pictures of the birds and scenery. Rosa asked Karin to pose in some.

Jim heard Rosa say, "Honey, you are so pretty without that frown!"

Jim knew she was trying to encourage the bitter girl. Karin smiled back awkwardly. She did not seem very comfortable with praise. Was there some experience that had turned this attractive person to anger?

Tatsuro and Ishido had a very expensive looking video camera and appeared to be in a high tech movie production. The two friends spoke rapidly in Japanese and were engrossed in the life of some insects at the base of a large rock.

Jim helped Weinberg and Stephen prepare the kitchen set up.

At dinner, everyone was bursting with chatter after their day of sequestered travel. Boisterous sharing of stories and amusing descriptions of other travels created a warm and safe shelter from the largeness of their surroundings. Weariness finally creeped upon the gathering. Gabriel made a fatherly suggestion that they get some rest. Everyone was so full of the experience of starting their safari that they were buoyed by natural adrenaline, but each agreed and one by one they bid the others good night.

Jim walked up to the jeeps to check one more time for anything he'd forgotten and was pleased to find his friend there. Weinberg's silhouette was framed by a basketful of stars spilled out across the forever blackness of the African night. He was smoking a pipe. The fragrance was sweet and aromatic.

Silently, the two men looked up in wonder at the unfamiliar constellations of the southern hemisphere.

Finally Weinberg spoke.

"Why did you come, Jim?"

"Oh, I thought I would make sure I didn't leave anything out in the jeep," Jim replied.

"No, not why did you come up here just now. Why did you come on the safari?"

Jim thought for a moment. "I'm not sure. You know I lost my job, already. I guess I didn't have much else going and thought it would be as good a time as any," Jim said looking down at his boots.

Weinberg pulled on his pipe. The glow of the tobacco coal lit his face in a dull, amber light.

"Jim, I have been watching you. You seem uncertain. You are obviously a very smart and talented man. We both know you will find other work. Probably a better job, with more money. Right?"

"That's true," said Jim. Headhunters had been calling him for some time before this all came down. They were offering him some pretty tempting opportunities with other employers, but he had been afraid to venture out on his own.

"Then why are you here, instead of home putting your career back in gear?"

Jim wanted to go back to his tent, but something made him stay.

"Weinberg, I feel like I am lost," he finally said. "I don't know what I want. I don't know what I feel. My wife says I am a louse and don't love her. I do, but I guess I don't show it. I can't seem to find the spark in life anymore..." Jim's voice trailed off.

"Somewhere, somebody is doing something you love to do and getting paid to do it," Weinberg said.

"That is very well and fine if you are clear on what you love to do!"

"Are you afraid?" asked Weinberg.

"Afraid of what?"

"You tell me."

Jim thought of the crippling fear that had haunted his every decision since childhood. How could Weinberg have nailed him so swiftly?

"Maybe," he said, hedging. "Things have always been kind of laid out for me. This is all very scary. I can't even seem to size up my chances to win because I don't know what game I'm in anymore."

"Often, confusion is a cloud brought on by our fears. Answers lie just beyond this veil," said Weinberg.

"So what is the answer?" said Jim. "Fear is fear. How do we stop it?"

"The only antidote for the poison of fear is action! Do what you fear the most and destroy the fear," said Weinberg.

"Oh, that's great! The reason we don't do stuff in the first place is exactly because we are afraid," said Jim, still using "we" instead of "I" intentionally.

"NO, it is NOT!" said Weinberg sharply. He continued in a seious tone, "I believe that in order to experience our true potential in life, we don't need much more information. We need courage and strength to face our self-limiting beliefs and fears. Then we can do the things we already know we ought to. That's the way, Jim."

Jim thought quietly about the power of the statement. He replayed it in his mind. Weinberg was dead right. The hairs on the back of Jim's neck tingled, causing a shiver. He felt electrified.

"What is the real thing, Jim?" Weinberg interrupted the silence.

"What do you mean?"

"The real thing. What is the most important thing in your life, what is second, what is third?"

"I never thought about it. I guess my family, my health, my career...," he trailed off.

"If someone were observing your life and writing a story about you, what would they say are the most important? How could someone tell what was the real thing to you?"

Jim thought hard about the idea of someone given

the task of describing his values by watching him go about his life. He wondered what they might see.

Weinberg paused, "Have you read *The Three Treasures'?"

"Yes, well, I have read the first treasure," he admitted, remembering he had told Benjamin he had read it all.

"Excellent!" said Weinberg. "That is the starting point for everything. You cannot make any decisions with any clarity without understanding the power of your mind to change your world."

Jim listened closely.

"Have you ever thought about prioritizing your values?" Weinberg asked.

"Why?"

"Imagine two people with the same three values you just mentioned: family, career, health. The first person says, 'Here are my priorities: number one is family, number two is health and number three is career.' The second person says career is first, health is second and family is third. Could you tell them apart?"

Jim thought. "Well, I guess. If the second person meant what he said, then he would always choose his career over his family or health and so on."

"Exactly!" congratulated the teacher. "You could spot them a mile away!"

Jim thought about his priorities and where he actually spent his time.

Weinberg continued, "Think about this trip, for instance. What are the priorities for Stephen and Gabriel?"

"I didn't know there was going to be a test!" protested Jim, attempting a little humor. They both laughed easily.

"Okay, I guess their priorities would be safety, time frame, and then adventure, in that order." Jim was already beginning to see. He continued, "That means their decisions would automatically be made based on these guidelines. Once the values are clear, the decision to take this road or that, where to camp and when to leave, are easily seen."

"Right, Jim!" encouraged Weinberg. "The Treasure of the Mind will help you gather wisdom, not more irrelevant data. Would you trade a life of meaning, joy, and understanding, for a trivial pursuit?"

"We'd best turn in. I've got a big surprise for you tomorrow. Are you interested in archeology?" asked Weinberg.

"You bet," said Jim, now curious. "What could be out here in the jungle?"

"You'll see tomorrow."

Jim thanked Weinberg for his insight and encouragement and headed for his tent. He re-read the Treasure of the Mind and made a few notes in his journal.

> *I feel like I can see the clouds beginning to clear in my mind,"* he wrote. *"I must stop worrying about what everyone else thinks and focus on what is really valuable to me. As I sharpen my mind and search for wisdom, the goal will be clear.*

They say the power and the path will open up only after the goal is clear.

Jim shut off his flashlight and lay flat out on his back, hands behind his head and listened, safe in his cocoon, to the strange and wonderful sounds of a night in the jungle. What in the world did Weinberg want to show him tomorrow?

THE SECOND TREASURE

There was a light and steady tapping noise in the tent. Jim slowly became aware of his surroundings and awoke to find that it was raining outside. The corner of the tent had a slight pull away from the border, and little drops were slowly forming and falling about every 5 seconds. Jim put his hand out to touch the water the way you touch a sore spot on your body for no reason.

He pulled on his pants and shoes and crawled out of the tent, tugging the wide brimmed hat down over his head. The rest of the camp was already gathered in the main cook tent, and conversation was lively. Jim returned from the "men's room" and joined the group.

Karin was arguing with Stephen about the proper way to make oatmeal while the others looked on with amusement at her seriousness about such a trivial matter. They were all doing an excellent job of enduring her particular nature, so far.

Jim poured himself a cup of coffee, added some powdered cream and pulled a campstool next to Weinberg. His new old friend gave him a smile and a pat on the back.

"Top of the morning!" Weinberg said in a happy voice. "Nice weather we're having, huh?"

"Well, at least it's not the monsoon," said Jim, commenting on the fact that although it was raining it was a gentle morning shower and not a downpour.

"Give it but a little time," said Gabriel to both Jim and the group. "The way of the rain in this valley is that the little brother rain comes first to announce his bigger brother is on the way! I fear that soon we will be experiencing much heavier weather. After breakfast I want us all to make some modifications to our campsite to prepare. You will notice I had already selected a high spot for your tents last night so you will need not move them. Let's make the jeeps secure and relax or hike in the area. We will not be traveling today."

Jim remembered his conversation with Weinberg about the priorities of the two guides. It seemed they planned safety first ahead of time. He looked over at Weinberg.

Weinber winked at Jim knowingly, gave his two thumbs up, and said, "Let's get the camp secure, then I'd like to show you that surprise."

As the two men worked together to double-stake the tents and make the camp extra safe from the predicted storm, suddenly there was a scream. It came from the area where the two women's tents were pitched.

It was Karin. She had tried to pull a second line across the back of the tent and succeeded in collapsing the whole thing on top of herself and was kicking the entire mess and shouting. Jim tried to keep silent but they all laughed out loud at the sight.

"I wonder what form of wild animal could be caught in this trap?" said Stephen with mock seriousness as he untangled the mess. "Oh, my! It is a man-eating oatmeal expert!" he smiled broadly as Karin's red tight-lipped face appeared from the folds of the tent. They all laughed loudly at his joke, and immediately Karin grinned bashfully and began to smile in spite of herself.

Weinberg asked Jim to gather his things for a hike and to meet him down by the jeeps. "Bring your journal and copy of The Three Treasures' too, Jim."

Jim wondered where they might be headed as he returned from the tent and made his way down the slope where Weinberg was already packing some supplies.

"Let's take along something to eat and prepare to be gone for the day," said Weinberg as he handed Jim several containers and packets of food and a first aid kit.

"Take a look at this."

Weinberg handed Jim an interesting electronic device.

"What is this?"

"It is an electronic location finder. You see, it uses satellites in orbit around the earth to beam back our coordinates. See, this is our exact location within a few feet. We can look this up on my map no matter where we are. There is absolutely no way we can get lost, even on the dark continent!" Weinberg beamed proudly at his high-tech toy.

The Safari Adventure Company

"What would Stanly and Livingstone paid to have one of those?" kidded Jim, admiring the amazing device. "I had no idea anything like that existed! Are you taking me into the wilderness?"

"You never know what you will run into out here. It is always best to prepare," he said with his thumbs up and winked.

It seemed to Jim that Weinberg was taking a lot of stuff for a day hike, but he shrugged it off as the kind of caution older people were known for. Jim was full of breakfast and more concerned with the load he would carry than the potential problems he may encounter. He remained silent, however, in deference to his new mentor.

They turned together and looked across the valley. The camp stood in a clearing on a slope about half way up the foothills that led to a large green mountain. Jim was used to seeing naked, rocky mountains. The dense foliage that covered the rise ahead made the mountain look soft and plush in the distance.

Although the sun was hidden by the low clouds, it was still rather bright. The mist from the floor of the valley gave the entire scene a surreal look. This was really Africa! Shockingly green and vibrantly alive. Brightly colored birds of cinnamon, amber, scarlet and pearl white called out from the bush and swooped from tree to tree. Their shrill voices echoed at different pitches from one end of the valley to the other.

Weinberg turned and pointed to a path that disappeared into the trees. They hiked ahead in intentional silence, absorbing the experience and turning to their own private thoughts. For over an hour they made their way on the remarkably clear lane gently climbing ever upward. Jim took in the sights and sounds and became immersed in the beauty of the incredible forest.

The rain was very different here because of the thick trees. It would hit the canopy overhead then collect on the leaves like a bucket. When they were full, the leaf would yield to the weight and spill huge drops with a loud PLOP onto the leaves and ground below. When one hit you, it felt like someone pouring a cup of water. You could hear the sound of it everywhere, but nowhere in particular as though it were up on the roof.

Occasionally they would come to a place where a hole would open up in the trees overhead. Jim removed his hat, and the misting rain would softly drift onto his face. It was cool and refreshing at this higher elevation. He rubbed the pure water on his eyes and face roughly, feeling the natural stimulation and energy.

Weinberg stopped abruptly and put his hand back, placing it on Jim's chest. Jim was looking down, his mind a million miles away from alertness. He looked up and his heart jumped with surprise when he saw why Weinberg had stopped. The path had taken a sudden right turn, and if he had not stopped, he would have gone right over a cliff!

They looked out together over a spectacular sight. There was a huge waterfall tumbling across the cliff on the opposite side of the canyon. Its peaceful flow at the headwaters reminded Jim of the slow way a rollercoaster takes the last few yards before screaming down from the top.

The waterfall must have been over five hundred feet down to the bottom where it fell into chaos and sprayed everywhere in the rocks below. The jungle had thanked the river by growing a thick bank of bush, trees, vines, and flowers, bathed in the mist of the spray. Dozens of monkeys scampered and played in the trees, safe from predators in this inaccessible place.

From there you could see the river wind lazily on through the canyon for miles before disappearing again into the paws of the jungle. Just then the sun broke through the darkening clouds and shot an incredible rainbow across the entire scene. The two men basked in the intense clarity and color of the moment.

Jim's heart began to slowly return to normal as Weinberg spoke his first words since they left the camp.

"There are some places on earth where the hand of God is clearly visible. This is mine, Jim."

Weinberg invited Jim to join him on a gigantic smooth rock that lay behind the path opposite the cliff. Jim sat his pack down and stretched out on the natural stone bench. He hadn't noticed how tired his legs were. It felt good to sit. They watched as the clouds reclaimed the little hole in the sky, and the rainbow faded. Even when it was gone, it seemed somehow indelibly etched in his memory.

Not wanting to rush the moment, Jim drank from his canteen and waited for Weinberg to speak.

"It has been seven years since I was here last. I feel ten bloody years younger right now because this place has not changed a fraction. It's funny, but even the smell is the same. Have you ever noticed how a smell triggers a memory?" he wondered aloud.

Jim thought about the smell of grapes. When he was a boy his mother had taken him to his aunt's house where she and her sisters made homemade grape jelly. The smell of grapes being cooked and the paraffin his mother and his aunts had used to seal the tasty delight was fresh in his mind though it was almost 35 years ago. His aunt had died 2 years later and Jim had forever associated the sweet smelling memory with her face.

"I can recall sitting here with Colonel Featherwood over twenty years ago and smelling those flowers." Weinberg pointed to a large bush with brilliant white flowers, their sweet, unique aroma permeated the place and settled into Jim's memory.

Jim leaned back on his pack and tried to drink it all in... the morning, the hike, the waterfall, the rainbow, the memories of his aunt and all the other memories that dominoed out of that one. First his gentle mother, then his stern father, came to him in words and stories viewed from the tender eyes of his childhood.

In his imagination, he looked down on the faces of his own children. Their childhood deeds and antics played like a movie in his thoughts. Soon his mind was miles away.

Opening his eyes, he tried to think carefully of something to say back to Weinberg, but there were no words in his vocabulary that would add a thing.

The rain had stopped. Weinberg pulled out his journal and began to write. Jim reached into his pack and found his copy of The Three Treasures. He opened it and began to read:

THE TREASURE OF THE HEART

Do nothing from selfishness or empty conceit, but with humility of mind let each of you regard one another as more important than himself; do not merely look out for your own personal interests, but also for the interests of others. Phillippians 2:3 & 4.

If you have heeded the words and employed the lessons thus far, you have embarked on the journey to carefully gather the most valuable treasures of life. You are to be applauded! Most never take the first step! You now need to understand what we could not suggest at the first.

The treasure of the mind has given you tools and

the information necessary to design a roadmap that will take you anywhere you choose to go. Up till now you have been in the process of gathering and focusing solely on your own lot. There is much more!

In order to begin to find the deeper fulfillment of life, we must return to the universe everything we have gained thus far. It is a principle of unquestionable truth that the only key that will unlock the most profound levels of wisdom and joy is borne of self denial. This awesome treasure is only discovered at the giving of all for the benefit of others.

There is a river that winds gracefully through a most beautiful land. It is populated by abundant life on both sides. It is the source of water, indeed life, for untold numbers of people and creatures great and small. At the end of the journey, the river runs into a very sad place.

You see, the river empties into a vast inland sea that has no outlet. Instead of the rich life that accompanies the river all along the way, the sea is desolate and bitter. In its waters travel no living thing whatsoever! Its shoreline is an alkaline wasteland with no living plant for miles and never the footprints of animals, for they cannot drink of it lest they die.

With no outlet it has become stagnant and poisonous. It takes in the best and devours it for itself and therefore it has earned, rightfully so, the name, The Dead Sea. This is the state of a person who takes and never returns to others. Thinking himself wise and successful, he is instead the victim of his own greed and selfishness.

Contrast the loving, giving person who seeks first to meet the needs of his fellows. His is a life of considerably more value than the former. He alone will know the joy of the smile of sincere appreciation, the warm caress of a thankful handshake, the embracing hug of gratitude of the one who has had an important need met.

Sadly, in our modern age there is an awful concept at work in the world at large. That is to think that if I give something away it is lost forever. Consider. If I give my time can I ever regain it? If I give my gold coins, my possessions, my attention, or honor, am I not required to go out and earn them again if I ever hope to be repaid? Though it seems so to the unsophisticated, the answer is a resounding NO!

In the fabric of the universe, all things given are retained in eternal time. Some are returned directly as our needs should call. Most reappear to us in the form of our own needs being met from an unpredictable source. This is the concept ancient scripture refers to as "Treasures in Heaven."

Here is the greatest miracle of all. When a person gives unselfishly to meet the needs of another, he does not receive back the equal portion. He actually gets back substantially more than he ever gave in the first! You may scoff here, and if you do, you are in the majority. The world has always laughed at wisdom. Only faith can witness the truth of this matter, and only trust can attempt to find out. In the end all giving results in abundant return far beyond the original investment.

As we love and give to others we find our own deepest needs for self esteem and power met and exceeded. As we turn and deprive our fellows of that which we could readily give, our real joy slips through our fingers into a Dead Sea.

We can hear your voice now saying, "The books and learning were easy to find and read. How shall we learn of this treasure? Where shall we find the path to its possession?" The answer is at once both simple and hard.

First, you must know that this answer is found down a road called The Via Dolorosa. Second, that the doorway that leads to this road is entered from any point around you where the choice between self-

ishness and generosity is to be made. You are making the choice daily. Choose life.

Jim folded the last page over to save his place and closed the book. It had never occurred to him that the old saying, "It is better to give than receive," might really be true. "Maybe that is why it got to be an old saying!" He thought to himself.

The image of the time he gave Claire that bike she wanted so badly popped into his mind. He could still remember the wide joyful eyes of his little daughter when she saw it under the Christmas tree at 6:30 in the morning. Tracey and he had done an excellent job of telling her they could not afford it and doubting Santa's ability to get the handlebars down the chimney.

He could almost feel his hands around her tiny shoulders in the soft teddy bear pajamas. Her grateful, slender arms once again were squeezing his neck as she said "Oh, thank you, Ookies," her nickname for him, in that little girl voice. A lump came to his throat as he closed his eyes to better capture the forgotten moment.

He looked up and saw that Weinberg was no longer writing but staring directly at him.

"I was reading about the Treasure of the Heart," Jim said quietly.

"Yes, the treasure of the heart. If I had understood that five years before I did, I could have saved so much pain and sorrow in my marriage."

"How do you mean?" asked Jim.

"I played the king of fools in the early years of my marriage," Weinberg offered immediately. "Oh, I was quite the gentleman in the courting stage. Once she was mine, however, I treated her like property. When she was sad, I was angry; when she was angry, I was mean; when she was lonely I was callous and uncaring.

"I always looked for what I could get from her. I always took, and I only gave to get my way. I married her so she could solve my problems. It never occurred to me that I had a responsibility to be her soul mate." Weinberg looked away now across the canyon toward the waterfall.

"What happened?" asked Jim after a moment.

"I read The Three Treasures.' I took the Safari, just like you are doing. I listened to Featherwood until he was blue in the face and when I finally got it, I went to her and begged her to forgive me," Weinberg offered candidly.

"And did she?" Jim asked.

"Absolutely not!" Weinberg said laughing. "After all the things I had said and done, I hardly believed myself. Yes, she was rightfully skeptical, but I determined to show her my newfound love was real. In the end, what we do speaks much louder than anything we say."

"How are things now," Jim pressed.

"She passed away two years ago, Jim. Part of the reason I have come back to the Safari this time is to fill the void that losing her has left in my life. To answer your question as it relates to your own marriage, I must tell you that we grew to love one another in the most profound way.

"Our relationship began to get real when I began to show her unconditional love. You see, Jim, in conflict resolution, it is incumbent upon the stronger to initiate peace. The weaker cannot initiate the peace; it won't work. It was up to me to take the first step. Frankly, it is my opinion that if any one person wants to save a marriage, it is possible. The only exceptions are mental problems or alcohol or drug addiction."

"I am very sorry that you have lost her, Weinberg. You must miss her very much," Jim offered softly.

"Yes, I miss her, but I am absolutely certain I will see her again in a short time in heaven. We have an appointment to keep, you know!" Weinberg smiled and gave his thumbs up. It was the kind of smile that you have to earn the hard way.

Jim thought about his own marriage and wondered if he were the strong one. Then a question came to mind from The Three Treasures.'

"Weinberg, what is the Via Dolorosa?"

"The Via Dolorosa is The Way of Suffering. It is the Latin name for the road that Jesus traveled from Pontius Pilate's court to Golgotha, The Place of the Skull, where he was crucified. It is symbolic for the path of self denial and absolute sacrifice of one's own self for the good of others.

"That is incredible," whispered Jim. "I didn't know that."

"The verses from the Bible at the front of the Treasure of the Heart are actually followed by the words: Have this attitude in yourselves which was also in Christ Jesus, who, although He existed in the form of God, did not regard equality with God a thing to be grasped, but emptied Himself, taking the form of a bond-servant, and being made in the likeness of men. And being found in appearance as a man, He humbled Himself by becoming obedient to the point of death, even death on a cross.'"

"Are these the exact words?" asked Jim, amazed at the quotation.

"Yes, the exact words," replied Weinberg.

"How did you learn the exact words?" asked Jim again.

"Well, actually, I memorized them. It has really worked to transform my life by renewing my mind. The most powerful way I have found to feed my mind is with real truth! When I look at what Jesus did for me, it is much easier to, in turn, do these much smaller kindness for others," said Weinberg.

Jim was lost for words. The ideas, the power of Weinberg's story, and the awesomeness of the location were data sensory overload for him. He turned toward the canyon and stared out across the sky. It had begun to rain again and, the clouds were growing darker.

Jim leaned forward and strained his eyes to verify a curious sight. There was a jeep far away across the canyon on the other side of the river moving along a dirt road. It was only there for a moment, then it disappeared silently around a turn and back into the jungle. Looking more closely he realized there was a clearing at the base of the falls on the other side and a winding path that went all the way to the top.

Jim traced the steep path in his mind and made a note to himself to ask Weinberg if it would be possible to hike up there. It would wonderful to view this compelling place from the top of the waterfall.

In a little while, Weinberg suggested they eat some lunch. Jim checked his watch and realized they had been gone over three hours. He was feeling quite hungry. The food tasted marvelous.

"So, this is what you wanted to show me?" asked Jim.

"No," smiled Weinberg, gathering up his things, "I am going to show you something very few living people have, or will ever see. Let's go."

ANCIENT ADVENTURERS

The narrow road along the canyon wound back into the bush and became almost invisible. There were a few places where the underbrush had begun to take back the trail. Broken branches and fresh machete marks told them someone had recently been through the trail. The going was mostly easy.

They hiked and cleared, crossed a small stream, and finally came to a wide open meadow. Weinberg pointed to a hill off to the left and said, "Over that hill is the second place I wanted you to see today." He then headed off toward the hill at a quicker pace. Jim hurried to keep up with the obviously excited Weinberg.

"He must be eager to see whatever it is," thought Jim. "He hasn't moved this fast since we left!"

Covering the short distance to the crest of the gentle hill, they reached the top together. Jim stared in astonishment.

There in the middle of the vast African wilderness sat what appeared to be a European monastery! Its unmistakable bell tower and spire rose up from the rich green valley. The walls and outbuildings were very much intact, although the grass and growth around the structure told the tale that there were no inhabitants.

Weinberg hesitated for only a moment to view the monastery from the hill and then began to make his way down the back of the hill and towards the building. Jim looked at Weinberg, looked at the monastery and slowly began to follow.

Approaching the building from the rear, they made their way around to the front. The courtyard was visible through the place in the wall where some great, wooden doors must have once hung. Instantly, Jim was struck with an overpowering sense of ancient history. He rubbed the goosebumps from his forearms as he walked across the stone courtyard toward a well and a stone bench in the center of the yard.

Although the monastery had been neglected for many years, there was a peaceful feeling of its unshakable consistency that seemed to say, "I am here and nothing can make me go away!"

"What in the world is this place doing way out here?" began Jim.

"If these old walls could speak...," Weinberg began and then paused. "It is just incredible, isn't it Jim?"

"Tell me about it, Weinberg," Jim asked.

"Featherwood came upon this place right after World War II while on a Safari with the club. In those days they really roughed it, you know, on foot with dozens of bearers and everyone carrying large amounts of gear. They explored and took photographs, quite dangerous really.

Anyway, Featherwood had heard tales of a group of monks from northern Africa in the second century who had ventured deep into the sub-continent as missionaries and had actually established a monastery South of the Congo River basin. When Featherwood came across this place he was thrilled. He actually made several trips here and brought some highly qualified people in to study it.

Featherwood brought me here on my first Safari and I saw the waterfall and this place all on the same day just as I am showing it to you. He told me what he believed to be true to the best of his research."

Jim sat spellbound and listened.

"It seems that a man named Justinius, who was a disciple of Andrew, one of the twelve disciples of Jesus himself, grew discontented with the selfish way the monks in North Africa and Europe had withdrawn to monasteries. He believed they were hiding far from anyone who did not believe The Way as Christianity was called in those days.

He went to Antioch, Constantinople, and Rome to seek the people who were considered the higher-ups of his faith and was very disappointed in the hindrances experienced by his brothers by their entanglement in the politics of the day. Stuck between the worldly cities and the reclusive monks, he gathered a group of followers and headed south to reach the people he had never seen and share the good news of his faith.

"That is absolutely incredible!" said Jim in amazement. He had always been fascinated with stories like this. What courage these men had. What incredible conviction! Jim had dreamed of being an archaeologist as a young boy staring at National Geographic magazines. Maybe it was this fascination that had first attracted him to the Safari!

"The fact that he was not killed is the greatest miracle! He had to cross the territory of cannibals and savages. In fact, this very land was inhabited by some of the fiercest tribes up until recent times.

They sat at the fountain and looked around at the painstaking construction that seemed so out of place in this land.

"The stones," Weinberg explained, " were hauled from the ruins of an ancient African city about a mile and a half away." The ruins were over 1,000 years B.C and made a convenient quarry. The monks fashioned them to resemble the familiar European counterpart. The result was odd sized and rough which made for a wild and natural look that Jim thought was at once strange and yet beautiful. The work that must have gone into this place was incredible. Weinberg said it had taken almost ten years to complete.

After they had rested Weinberg suggested they take a look around. They crossed the courtyard and entered a door at the side that led into the monks' living quarters. Weinberg produced a flashlight from his backpack and led the way.

The monks had built small, simple cells. They also developed an ingenious ventilation system. It was remarkably cool and comfortable despite the African heat and humidity. Along the wall where a small writing table must have been, sharp angular letters were carved in the stone.

"The monks were given to writing a favorite scripture in their rooms. Usually a life verse' or a special scripture that meant something unique to them," said Weinberg.

"I guessed they weren't writing graffiti!" said Jim playfully. He was having a wonderful time and felt like a great archaeologist. What a privilege it was to actually see and touch something so few would ever experience.

"Look here, Jim," said Weinberg shining his flashlight on some other writing above the Latin inscription. "Featherwood translated and wrote the words in English."

Jim looked down to see the words, "I can do all things through Christ who strengthens me," written in black above the carefully chiseled Latin verses.

They made their way along the halls and entered the chapel. Jim drew a quick breath of surprise as he looked up at the large, two story room. The monks had constructed an absolutely beautiful church here in this desolate place. The short railing in front of the platform was made from highly polished, dark brown stone.

The walls were drawn with pictures of Bible stories from the Old and New Testament times. The colors had faded, but still you could clearly see the images of angry Moses parting the sea, Daniel patiently praying in the den of lions and the gentle Christ on his knees washing the feet of his astonished disciples.

A sculptured statue of Jesus on the cross surveyed the room from high above and behind the stone pulpit. The stone benches were lined in little rows. The place must have been able to seat almost 100 people. Weinberg sat on the back row and silently looked around, as if admiring an old friend. Jim sat reverently beside him. They looked like two church visitors who had arrived early and were waiting for services to begin.

All at once the dim room exploded in a rainbow of bright colored light! There were streams of sapphire blue, ruby red, gold and emerald coming in from all around piercing the thick stone walls.

"The natives brought quartz pieces to the monks as gifts when they first arrived," Weinberg explained, chuckling at the expression on his astonished companion's face.

When they began to build the chapel the monks inserted them in the walls and found quite by surprise that sunlight pierced them in a stained glass effect. The monks had always planned to light it with candles. Since the Monastery has its back to the East, this chapel literally glows in the early morning sunlight."

"This is extraordinary, Weinberg. How many times can you say Wow!?'" asked Jim, looking around. "Why are there so many seats for a handful of monks?"

"Well, the monks were not here to hide from the world. They came to teach The Way,' as they called their faith, to the people. There were many converts, and in a few years the chapel could not hold them all at the same time." said Weinberg. "This was actually quite a bustling community it its day."

"How did Featherwood learn so much about the group?" asked Jim. "There is not that much information on these walls."

"Featherwood was quite the amateur archaeologist. He excavated and uncovered records in a trash heap nearby. His greatest prize, he told me was how he found part of the journal of Justinius while digging through a separate section a short distance from the monastery. That is where he learned much of what we know today. It is in a lovely, antique glass display case back at the lodge where we met," said Weinberg.

"I believe," he continued, "this is a living example of the Via Dolorosa. These men gave their lives to serve others. They abandoned everything familiar for a cause higher than themselves. What joy they must have known. What incredibly valuable lives they lived!"

The light faded as the sun ducked back behind a

cloud, reminding the men they had an hour and a half hike back to the camp. So they reluctantly gathered their things and prepared to leave. They turned to cross the front of the chapel when Jim tripped and fell face first across a coffin shaped wooden crate.

He sat on the floor and rubbed his shin, glaring at the offending box. It was pried open and the barrel of a gun and the stock and sight of another were easily visible through the opening. It was then they noticed in the dimming room that laid along the boxes across the front of the chapel were ivory tusks of all sizes.

"The monastery is being used by poachers," said Weinberg sadly. "Let's get out of here—we have a long way to go to get back to the camp."

As they crossed the courtyard by the fountain near the entrance, they both heard the sound of a jeep, gunning the engine. Jim peered around the wall and saw a band of five fierce looking men wearing dirty, military style camouflage fatigues and carrying weapons. They were arguing excitedly and heading straight for the monastery. Weinberg motioned Jim back in the chapel.

"They must have a road cut back to a village somewhere. There is no way for us to make it across the clearing and head up the path to camp without being seen," he whispered. "Let's circle to the monk's cells, and I will show you a place where we can slip out the back and into the bush. Follow me!"

The Ancient Adventurers

Running back into the monastary, they moved quickly and quietly along the darkening corridor and exited through a narrow passageway into the dense jungle along the side of the monastery. The sound of the men arguing in heavily accented English grew louder.

Apparently one of the men was very unhappy with the other over some matter of money. They were using the most vulgar language to describe what they would do to each other if the issue was not settled to their satisfaction. The other men were laughing at the fight and egging the two combatants on.

Jim and Weinberg found it very tough going in the growth around the back of the monastery. They were trying to be quiet, yet make progress towards the path back to the camp. The poachers disappeared inside the chapel, and the whole area became eerily silent.

Weinberg turned to Jim and said, "We are going to have to try to get back to camp before dark. Gabriel knows where I have taken you. If we do not return, he will set out after us in the morning and he might run into these miserable fellows. I cannot run as fast as you, but I can make pretty good time. Let's make a dash across the clearing now and try to get over the hill before we're seen!"

"Let's do it," said Jim, his pulse racing at the danger and excitement. He did not understand the gravity of the situation, but was frightened at the unknown and ready to get back to camp.

"Do you have your pistol, Jim?" asked Weinberg.

"Sure I do," said Jim warily. Turning to Weinberg with a concerned look on his face he said, "I can't shoot anyone — you can't be serious."

Weinberg stared back at Jim silently.

"It's in my backpack," Jim answered the unasked question as he fetched the gun and slipped it in his belt.

The instant they stepped out of the underbrush, but before they could run, the entire band of men came around the back of the monastery and into the clearing. Jim and Weinberg lurched to a halt and backed quickly into the bush unseen. There they crouched just inside the foliage and watched as the men built a brush pile for a bonfire.

The poachers were drinking whiskey and laughing as they prepared for some kind of African barbecue. Jim and Weinberg were trapped between the wall of the monastery and the thick jungle. If they tried to work their way into the jungle, the noise and motion in the thick underbrush would give away their presence. They could only sit helplessly and watch as the poachers lit the bonfire and drank as darkness fell.

The two men silently shared the rations Weinberg had so wisely brought along. They talked quietly between themselves, and, although they were in a tough spot, it was not all that impossible. The plan was to wait until darkness when the poachers went to sleep. They could then steal across the camp and make some progress up the path, then high-tail it back to camp at dawn. Surely the drunken poachers were not early risers. They lay back against a tree and waited for the darkness.

Jim awoke to the sound of furious screaming. Weinberg and he had fallen asleep. Night had come. The bonfire was giving off a macabre, orange glow to the scene before them.

The two men who had argued earlier were now face to face, quite intoxicated and literally shrieking at each other. They had rediscovered the unsettled money question and were threatening bloody murder if not made whole. The taller man was brandishing a machete, while the shorter one was trying in vain to spit on him. Both men were wobbly and hopelessly drunk.

Jim looked out at the scene before him in absolute disbelief. Still sleepy, it seemed as if it were a dream. He was in the African jungle hiding from outlaws. Their shadows leaped across the monastery wall in giant caricatures of villains amplified by the flickering firelight. If he and Weinberg were discovered, who knows what might become of them. Jim's life was on the edge of its seat!

Suddenly, the man with the machete lunged forward. He leveled the machete towards the throat of the spitter. Had he been sober, he would have severed his head. Instead he raked him across the chest with a striking blow.

No sooner had the machete made its pass when

three gunshots cracked the air.. Their sharp clapping echoed into the jungle. The man with the machete jerked violently and fell back into the fire but not before pulling out a revolver and firing helplessly at no one. One of the bullets streaked into the jungle just past Jim's ear as he and Weinberg buried themselves in the dirt.

The machete man's body twisted in the fire in a sickening way as he died. The bullets in his belt began exploding at random propelling his assassins for cover. This they found absolutely hilarious and squealed with bizarre laughter at the fireworks show. They found joy in the killing their own companion!

The explosions ceased and the body settled, slowly undulating into the ashes. The poachers tended to their wounded friend and laughed and drank some more. Apparently the machete man was not much liked by the group and was good riddance. They settled down and proceeded to get seriously drunk.

Weinberg and Jim had no opportunity to escape. Tired as they were, they drifted in and out of consciousness as the bandits randomly sang and fired their guns into the jungle like cattle rustlers. Eventually the entire group collapsed on the ground and began snoring loudly.

After waiting to be sure the poachers were unconscious, Jim pulled Weinberg up from his spot. The older man had gotten sore and cramped in hiding. They crept quietly past the murderers, carefully averting their eyes from the smoldering cremation fire and disappeared over the hill just as the sky began to promise morning.

AFRICAN STORM

Though it had rained steadily off and on all through the previous day, it had never really stormed as the guide had predicted. The men proceeded hurriedly back to the camp with the sound of thunder and occasional streaks of lightning punctuating their steady footsteps.

"Gabriel will be on the path looking for us right now. We are so lucky to get out of there before he got to the monastery. He might have stumbled right on top of that crew," said Weinberg, looking up at the threatening sky. "How disappointing to find the old church being home to such a wretched lot!"

They paused for a short moment to catch their breath at the stone bench atop the waterfall view. It was absolutely breathtaking to see the black boiling clouds push up the valley. Filled with lightning and peals of thunder as they advanced toward the hikers, they looked like a chariot of some mighty mythological warrior. Jim thought how easily the ancient and uneducated could be impressed to invent legends that would explain such a powerful display of nature.

"Why didn't we take everyone along to see the

monastary?" Jim asked a question he had pondered, but hadn't had time to ask.

"Gabriel and Stephen were going to bring them up tomorrow," Weinberg replied. "They were exploring another area yesterday, and I asked if we could come up here alone. Old time's sake, you know." Weinberg pulled his electronic location finder our of his backpack. It was smashed and useless.

"I must have crushed it sometime during the ducking and hiding," he said, looking down at it sadly. "Nevertheless, I know this path very well. We won't be needing this fancy compass anyway," he said, tucking the useless box back in his pack.

The storm was progressing, and Gabriel would be searching for them along the way so they pushed on back toward the camp. Weinberg was strong. Despite the lack of sleep and stress of the terrible night before, the men moved with energy and purpose.

Jim's mind began to wander as they wound along the path. He remembered the day he found the Safari advertisement in his desk drawer and thought it was probably a bunch of old men in fatigues drinking cocktails and sleeping in campers. He laughed in spite of himself. Would he have gone if he had known about the danger of last night?

They drew closer to camp and still no Gabriel. Weinberg thought it odd and said so. Perhaps there was a more alarming problem. He couldn't imagine what. There were very strict guidelines of protocol for missing hikers.

At once, the jungle opened up and they could clearly see the the path down to the jeeps ahead. Weinberg stopped, then backed up a couple of steps. Jim stood beside him and looked down the hill in horror. There was only one jeep and it had been set on fire and was now smoldering and destroyed! Farther across the clearing lay the destruction of the campsite. It was ransacked. Supplies, tents, and pieces of clothing were scattering in the rising wind.

"Weinberg, what is going on?" asked Jim

"Something is terribly wrong here, Jim," said Weinberg, his jaw set as he headed down hill.

Jim was the first to see the bullet casings near the campfire. Weinberg found the body. Gabriel had been shot several times. His cold body had been dead for hours.

They called out for the others and searched the area all around the camp, but no one answered. There were footprints on the jeep trail that led off in the direction that they would have continued the safari. It appeared as though the others had gone ahead on foot. They found some of the supplies and parts of the tents scattered around in the bush. As they gathered what was salvageable, they talked.

"Do you think the poachers did this?" asked Jim.

"Why in God's name would someone have to kill like this to protect their illegal turf," said Weinberg, answering his question. "They must be trying to scare off visitors to the area."

"What about the local game wardens? How can they get away with this?"

"The odds of whoever did this ever being caught are very slim. You saw last night the world these people live in. They are more likely to kill the game wardens than be arrested and brought to trial!" Weinberg replied.

Lightning streaked across the sky and the wind threw the leaves into a shiver. Jim grabbed hold of his hat as the rain began again this time with larger and heavier drops. The storm Gabriel had predicted was coming, and it was going to be big.

The men decided not to remain there for fear of the return of the poachers. They struggled down the jeep road until the rain and wind drove them deep into the jungle. There, wedged between two large trees, they pulled a piece of tent over their weary bodies and heavy packs and huddled down to ride it out. The crude tent was dry and dark. Hidden from the road, the exhausted men lay back against their packs and slowly fell asleep as the sound of the storm droned on into the night.

Hopelessly Lost

Mountain peaks bathed in a golden-pink sunset descending into a lush emerald forest. Vibrantly colored birds and flora abounding. Ruby and sapphire light from crystal gems imbedded in an ancient chapel wall. Greedy and vile men drinking, fighting, and shooting guns in the firelight. Jim sat down in the grass. His hand touched something warm and wet. A crimson stain of blood weeped slowly off his outstretched fingers onto the body below. Body? Body!

Jolted from a nightmare, Jim bolted upright. Trying to stand, he caught his arm on the rope which had been strung from the trees to create a makeshift lean-to for the night. Totally disoriented he stumbled, and fell backward onto the ground landing right on top of Weinberg.

"Jim, what in heaven's name are you doing?" cried Weinberg.

"Oh, man!" Jim shouted apologetically as the last twenty four hours tumbled back into reality.

"Here! Here! Jim, settle down now. It's okay—we're all right," consoled Weinberg politely, rubbing his ribs.

"Gosh, I'm sorry. Are you hurt? asked Jim, as he scrambled to his feet.

"No. I'm fine. You do make an interesting alarm clock though!" He rolled over, sat up and gave his thumbs up sign.

Jim patted his new mentor on the shoulder squeezing an apology and appreciation. Jim was never one to show affection, but, it came spontaneously. Weinberg put his hand on Jim's and patted a quick acceptance.

"Here, have a bit of breakfast." Weinberg handed him some dried fruit.

"Yeah...good idea," said Jim. "Do you have any bacon and eggs in there?" He asked, smiling weakly.

Jim put some of the fruit in his mouth and began to think about their next move. The fruit tasted sweet. Jim recalled how Weinberg loaded them up with supplies and how he had almost foolishly balked at taking the extra weight.

"Okay, Jim, what do you say we hike back toward the campsite and see what supplies are left. We'll use the sun as our guide during the day. That is, when we can see it." Weinberg looked up at the heavy foliage.

We don't know where everyone else has disappeared to. Maybe we'll run across them later. More importantly, we have to be on the look-out for those poachers. We'll keep to the road, but we'll have to be ready to bail into the forest if we hear jeeps. It's just too risky to strike out through the jungle.

"Right," said Jim as he busied himself with the task. "You're right—let's get started. Best thing to do now."

It was taking longer than they thought it would to find the road. It soon became obvious they had cut their way deeper into the bush than they realized. Perhaps they were all turned around. Maybe they were not heading back to the road at all, but farther into the jungle. Jim began to silently worry.

After several hours it became crystal-clear. Neither man needed to say a word. They were utterly lost. Weinberg never showed any signs of fear or worry. He had maintained a positive attitude and reassured Jim they would find one of the roads soon. He encouraged him to press on and keep his eyes open. As they sat on a log by a small stream, Weinberg bowed his head and folded his hands. Jim knew he was praying.

"I hope he throws one in for me!" thought Jim.

Finally Weinberg looked up. His eyes were moist with tears.

"Weinberg, are you scared?" asked Jim, a little surprised.

"No," laughed Weinberg, wiping his eyes with his blue bandanna, "I just began to think about my wife. I felt as if I heard her voice. It was strange how the sensation was so real. She was saying not to worry. She was always such a great encourager to me whenever I faced a tough challenge. I guess I just got a little emotional. Happy, though!" He smiled and gave a little thumbs up and winked a reddened eye.

The Safari Adventure Company

Their spirits lifted when they saw a familiar looking hill through the trees. They decided to press on toward it. The struggle through the undergrowth had begun to take a toll on Weinberg, and his weariness showed. With the next swing of his machete, exhaustion overtook him and it slipped out of his hand and flew into the air. Jim watched as the machete fell into the shallow ravine they had been walking along.

"Let me go down and get it for you," Jim insisted.

Slipping the backpack off his shoulders, Jim began to lower himself carefully down the side of the ravine. Sighting the machete with its handle sticking out from a bush a few feet away, he quickly grabbed it and started back up the incline.

As he looked up to get his grip on another vine, his eyes locked with those of an enormous black panther! It was poised and ready for attack, halfway between Jim and the top of the embankment. The muscular onyx body and the intense concentration in the panther's gleaming stare froze Jim in his tracks.

The hair on his arms and neck stood on end. He thought he was afraid of snakes, but this was a million times worse. The yellow eyes of the huge cat were ice cold and hypnotic as it stood, silent, just a few yards away.

Down the hill Weinberg's voice came softly. "Jim, just stand still. Don't move," he whispered hoarsely.

Jim's nightmare came to life as a blue and orange parrot flew noisily out of the trees just above the panther's head. The panther, startled, sprang sideways enough for Weinberg's carefully calculated shot to miss the cat and shatter bark from the tree beside it.

Without waiting, Weinberg came crashing down the hill, shouting to draw the panther's attention onto him. It worked. The panther turned from Jim and toward the attacker. Weinberg came half running, half sliding, down the hill directly between Jim and the panther, shouting and firing the pistol as he came.

In instant reflex the panther unleashed a soul wrenching scream, crouched and sprang at its attacker. The weight of the great cat drove Weinberg to the ground. He continued to fire the pistol into its belly as the vicious killer tore at his face and throat with both spiked claws.

Jim ran to the brawl. With a guttural cry, he slammed the machete with all his might onto the panther's neck. Blood shot everywhere as the blow shattered the cat's shoulder bone. The wounded panther, still astride Weinberg, spun around and swiped at Jim, teeth bared and hissing. The razor-sharp claws ripped across Jim's chest and knocked him down the ravine again.

Instinctively, returning to its work, the still-powerful creature sunk its huge fangs into the neck of its victim, choking off Weinberg's scream. The only sound was the "click-click-click" of the empty revolver as Weinberg continued to helplessly squeeze the trigger. In one great violent twist the panther snapped

Weinberg's neck like it had done so many times before to antelope victims.

Jim, scrambled back up the hill, and drew his pistol. In a leap he was only a few feet from the mauling terror. He raised the pistol and fired. The bullet ripped into the black panther's neck above the machete wound. The frenzied panther unable to walk from the broken shoulder and already carrying several of Weinberg's bullets, tried to rush Jim. Bleeding badly, it began crawling toward Jim, the object of its pain, blood dripping from its gaping mouth.

Jim deliberately fired one shot...two shots into the killer's brain. As the second round slammed into its skull, the panther rolled over, clawing the air slowly.

Weinberg's body had rolled under a bush. Jim pulled the bush aside and saw his friend's horribly mutilated body. Lifting a blood soaked wrist, he felt for a pulse, already knowing there would be none.

Panic, anger, and fear took turns sending electric jolts into Jim's solar plexus in shock waves. In a white-hot anger he looked back at the dying panther, re-loaded the gun and fired every round into the now still beast.

He returned to Weinberg and knelt gently by his friend, stunned by the absolute brevity of their relationship. There was no good-bye. No last words to treasure. Should he bury him? How? He had no shovel!

The jungle had gone wild during the gunshots and the fight. Now the screaming birds and monkeys once so loud and raucous became very still. Eerily feeling eyes on his back, Jim turned slowly and saw another panther, glaring at him from behind a log just a few yards away!

Jim backed himself awkwardly down the ravine. Stumbling on a limb he fell to the bottom of the ridge. In shock and for fear of his life, he jumped up and ran as fast as he could.

Falling, running, falling, he tore through the bush until he thought his heart would burst. He finally collapsed. Up in only a moment, he ran again until exhaustion overtook him. He let himself roll to the ground and crawled helplessly under a huge fern.

In the growing darkness and seclusion of the foliage, he struggled to maintain consciousness. Pain seared through every inch of his tortured body. The terrible stinging cut from the panther's clawing, forgotten as he ran, now sliced across his chest in waves. The bruises and cuts from falling and being slashed by the jungle demanded relief. But, there was no relief.

Hoping against hope that the other panther would not track him, but unable to move on, Jim lay panting under the great bush like a doomed rabbit. Darkness swept across the jungle as he pulled the leaves across his body, curled up in a ball, and closed his eyes.

During the night, an army of ants had found the leftover dried fruit in Jim's shirt pocket. He awoke in a panic to brush their trail off his neck. He hated and cursed the ants in the clear light of the dawn. He was hungry, too.

He forced himself to make a decision and take action. He could not lie here and wait for help or death! He couldn't allow himself to think about Weinberg, not yet. Swallowing hard he came out from under the waxy green fern and looked around.

He wasn't sure what time of day it was, only that it was daytime by the amount of light diffusing through the trees. He thought about eating the fruit ants and all, but brushed them away first and nibbled carefully at the morsel.

Calmer and rested, he took an inventory. All he had was the revolver and his pocketknife. He knew he must go back to the top of the ravine and retrieve his backpack of supplies. He would have to overcome the idea of what he would find there in order to survive.

Following the broken limbs of yesterday's flight Jim proceeded cautiously, the small revolver drawn and ready. Making his way up the bank he recognized the ravine where the battle had taken place. Peering cautiously over the embankment, Jim saw no sign of Weinberg or, thankfully, the slain panther. The jungle had removed them. Relieved, yet lonelier than ever, he searched for the backpacks. The lost machete lay a few yards away.

Jim's bright blue backpack was right where he had laid it yesterday. Weinberg's dark red pack was lying halfway down the ravine. The lightweight aluminum frame was badly bent either by Weinberg's fall or the rushing panther. Jim ran his fingers over the bend gently, feeling the loss of his mentor. Looking inside the pack he saw some packets of food, a flashlight and a small worn Bible. Jim tucked them in his pocket without thinking, grabbed his own gear, and took cover between a grouping of tree trunks to think.

"What in the world am I going to do?" he said out loud listening nervously to the smallness of his own desperate voice. The smell of the jungle, so humid and musty from the rain, mingled with the flowers and animal musk that permeated everything. His mind was silent and empty. As he sat between the huge, gnarled tree roots, he began to differentiate between the noises from the forest. They had been blended before into a dull sameness. He listened.

Rustling foliage from small burrowing animals, chimpanzee laughter, and a symphony of bird calls greeting the morning came to his ears one at a time. As he raised his eyes upward to look into the intertwined canopy of heavily weighted branches and thickly woven vines, he noticed he had an audience. Four small white-faced monkeys were watching him in amusement. Their heads tilted this way and that as if they wondered what manner of entertainment they were about to enjoy.

Jim let out his breath slowly, relaxed his shoulders, and smiled weakly. Then he sank back against the tree trunk and closed his eyes for a moment. His mind began to pick up speed.

At once he was painfully aware of how alone he was among the other species in the forest. There seemed to be no other humans in existence. Then his mind flashed a scene from an old Twilight Zone episode where a submarine commander was the only survivor of a nuclear war. The captain had walked through town after town searching for another person.

Ten thousand terrors paraded their awful outcomes before him. What had become of the others in his safari group? Had they even survived the poacher at-attack? Where were the scouts from the Safari Adventure Company? Was anyone even looking for him?

The crackling of a large, rotted branch breaking off and landing with a thud nearby brought Jim back to reality. He must concentrate on finding a way back to the compound. Jumping to his feet, he secured his backpack, got a firm grip on Weinberg's machete, and began clearing his way toward the east and the hill they had seen the day before.

He had been hard at work for probably thirty minutes, and he felt he was making good headway. He could see that the forest looked lighter ahead and picked up his pace in hope. Maybe it was a road or at least a clearing. His ears were straining to hear any sound of rescue or predator as he chopped and tried to ignore the continual noise from the forest.

As he parted two large palm leaves, Jim was nearly

Hopelessly Lost

blinded by the amount of light. A road! He had found a road! He stumbled happily onto the red, dusty tire tracks and closed his eyes thankfully.

Ah, Benjamin would be so proud of him now! He'd made it through the training. He'd come to Africa, been pushed to the limit, and he had found the main road again!

Benjamin. He seemed light years away. Jim's idea of a safari and visiting was so idyllic compared to the ordeal he'd gone through. He suddenly became aware of the moment and the incredible power of his own personal adventure.

"Everyone has their own adventure," the Dutchman had said, talking about green-peas. "Each person will see this thing through their own unique eyes."

Jim definitely had his own story to tell. He had to make it back! He would survive and live to tell!

Looked up toward the sun he tried get a bearing of his location. Tenderly touching the caked blood on his shirt from the chest wound, he began walking east. After a half mile, Jim saw something up ahead on the road. Forgetting any danger, he sprinted toward it.

He stopped suddenly with surprise. It was the remains from the group's camp that he and Weinberg had found before. Not much was left behind by the poachers. Remembering where he had found Gabriel's body, Jim avoided looking that direction.

Well, at least this meant he knew where he was. Maybe he could find some more supplies. He began rummaging through the demolished tents.

After being hidden by the dense jungle for so many hours, Jim felt very exposed in the openness of the campsite. Looking up and over his shoulder, he wondered if anyone was watching him. He wasn't sure which he was more frightened, of the possibility of another panther or the poachers. Realizing the dangers again, he scrambled to his feet and darted for the forest's camouflage at the side of the road, his arms full of new-found supplies.

Sitting in the bush, he ate thankfully from the tins and packets he had salvaged from the dismal camp site. He decided to head back up the road to the west. They had only driven for a day from the Lodge at the Lake of Stars. Surely there had been some type of search started after the loss of radio contact with the group. Besides, it was mostly downhill and would be more familiar than the unknown route farther along to the halfway station.

Jim cleaned and dressed the wound on his chest. The blood had made it look a lot worse than it actually was. He bandaged it and changed into a clean shirt from one of the bags at the campsite.

Feeling more confident, he carefully packed up the things he decided to take. At least he still had his special hat! What a memento it would be in the years to come!

He walked out of the jungle and headed west, back toward the lake. Past the burned out jeep, he stopped at the top of the ridge to look back at the valley. How beautiful it had seemed as he and Weinberg pulled up that first sunset afternoon. He remembered how Weinberg had grabbed the wheel to keep them from hitting the jeep ahead. He smiled sadly, then turned to walk down the hill to the west.

After walking only a few paces, there came a sound like a jeep engine off in the distance. Jim could not tell which direction it was coming. From the west, yes! It was coming from the west! It must be some sort of rescue team from the lodge. Jim stood in the middle of the road and waited. Soon the jeep was in sight. As it drew closer Jim began to wave his arms. The figures in the jeep pointed toward him and the sound of the engine said the vehicle was speeding up.

The jeep slipped out of sight around a bend at the bottom of the hill and reappeared, now much closer. Jim could see the logo of the Safari Adventure Company on the front of the jeep, but, something was wrong. Something was terribly wrong. The faces of the men in the jeep were suddenly clearer and there was a man standing in the back with something in his arms.

It was the poachers! Jim froze in terror as the man in the back raised the high powered rifle to his face and fired! The jeep lurched as it grazed a rock, and the shot spattered the red dirt a few yards behind Jim. Terrified, he ran back past the burnt out jeep and into the jungle until he found himself on the trail that led back to the Mission.

"Oh, no!" He panicked. "This is the road they came down after killing the guide!"

Jim pushed off the path and deeper into the trees. The poachers stopped the jeep at the edge of the jungle, and all the men leapt to the ground and followed. They shouted instructions in some unknown African dialect and fired their weapons in the direction they had last seen Jim.

Running for his life, he felt like a frightened, hunted animal. The poachers were having great sport. They were expert hunters and much better at making their way through the jungle. Jim was terrible at both and worse at being an elusive prey.

Every time he thought he was safe, he would pause to let his heart stop pounding only to hear the sound of the men approaching again.

"They are tracking me!" he thought and another wave of helpless terror swept over him.

It seemed like hours when he finally came to a fast moving narrow stream. He jumped down into the water and made a snap decision to go to the left. If he was right, this would take him back and eventually lead him to the road heading east to the halfway station. He would follow the stream for a while to hide his trail from the trackers and then change direction. Maybe the water would throw them off like it did hound dogs in the movies!

Leaving the water about a half mile down, he pushed ahead toward the west. Finally he stopped and sat down with his back against a tree and tried to collect himself. He closed his eyes as his breath came down to normal. So tired. He felt sleepy. Just a little rest. He drifted off.

The sharp crack of a snapping twig woke him suddenly. He opened his eyes to another world. It was almost dark. He stood suddenly to his feet. Peering into the bush he strained in the bluish gray of the dusk to see if poacher, panther or any other danger were nearby. Jim eased the pistol out and released the safety. His throat was too tight to swallow. He had no desire at all to shoot anyone, but in the dim twilight, half mad with fear, he was ready to deal with any situation with lethal force.

As his eyes adjusted to the shadows, he saw him! The lone poacher was about 30 yards away crouching in the bush. He was wearing a dark brown baseball cap and fatigues and was raising his rifle slowly to his eye. In the split second that changes so many lives, Jim pointed the pistol and fired three times directly toward the poacher. Out of the corner of his eye he saw the man roll to his side, whether from being shot, or to take cover, Jim did not wait to see.

Still holding the pistol, Jim ducked down and grabbed his backpack, then carefully backed around the tree and sprinted off in the direction he had been heading. He ran a few steps toward through the trees when all at once he was staring into an endless valley and teetering on the edge of a gigantic cliff! He had already lost his balance and could not stop. Jim felt his stomach lurch into his throat as he fell over the edge!

He thrashed his arms wildly to find something to grab, but there was nothing but air. It was too fast to scream. He fell for what seemed like an eternity, then felt himself crashing into the branches of a tree and slamming down to the ground with a thud—now rolling and sliding at incredible speed down the hill.

The last thing he remembered was his head slamming into something solid, sending him into blackness as he continued to deadfall, straight down the mountain.

THE THIRD TREASURE

The tall grass swayed gracefully in the gentle breeze of another morning on the golden savannah. The first beams of dawn awoke the local neighborhood, and the sound of life was up again and about its business. The sky was deep blue and clear except for a lone vulture that had begun to circle hopefully. Its potential breakfast was lying face down at the bottom of the steep hill that emptied out on to the wide grassy plain.

Jim was awakened by the soreness of his shoulder and ribs. He rolled over on his back. Staring straight up into the sky, the madness of his situation came back to him one more time. He looked up at the mountain and saw the bluff from where he must have fallen. It made him sick to see that he had dropped over one hundred feet before hitting the ground! He had luckily crashed through the branches of some trees that cushioned his fall. Otherwise he would surely have died.

He thought of the man he had fired his pistol on the night before. Was he dead, wounded, or worse, still looking for him? The poachers must have given up and assumed Jim could not have survived the fall, that is if they even came this far. Jim was beyond caring about the poachers, though.

This was worse than any nightmare, but there was no use in running, he thought. Instead of jumping up and trying to frantically take some foolish action, Jim just lay there and thought. I am absolutely lost. I am tired, weak and hurt. He put his hand on an enormous painful lump on the top of his head and then on his aching shoulder. He arched his back to relieve his ribs, and the sting of the panther cuts reported their presence.

"I am so hungry! My backpack must be gone. I could actually starve out here!" His fears ran wild, creating endless scenes of destruction. Just then he sensed the shadow of the vulture pass overhead and realized he was looking at him! "Oh, great! I have already been assigned to nature's garbage machine."

Lying there wrapped in an endless wave of self pity and fear, something new happened to Jim—something he thought he had forgotten how to do.

He began to cry.

It welled up in him from deep within his soul. At first the slow coughing, then a moaning sob, and then he turned back over on his face and let go. He cried like a baby. Drawing handfuls of grass into his blood streaked, white-knuckled fists, he writhed and wailed, beyond comfort.

What a fool to come to Africa at a time like this in his life! What foolish choices had led him to lose his job. Why in the world had he made so many mistakes in his life? He wept and thought of them all. Every single one. He longed to hold his wife, his daughter, his son.

The Third Treasure

"I have been a total failure as a husband, as a father, oh, dear God, as a man! He wanted to just give up, but there was no one to accept his surrender. That just made it worse.

His salty tears stung the scratches on his face. He rubbed them into his eyes with his fist. Bitterly, he cursed God, nature, his life, and the stinking, sorry Safari Adventure Company. He wanted to die.

Turning on his side again, he glimpsed something in the grass. A jackal hesitated a moment then darted away. He had been drawn by the sound of his crying. Jim got to his knees, then got to his feet, and stood in the waist high grass.

He traced his fall down the hillside and found his backpack. A little farther ahead he was excited to see his soft, wide brimmed hat.

"Hello, old friend," he said sadly, glad to see anything familiar.

Placing it tenderly on his sore head, he looked around at the wide plain. Somewhere he could hear the sound of water. Realizing how very thirsty, he was he moved in the direction of the sound. The grass sloped down to a beautiful river, moving along at an easy pace. It was crystal clear and inviting. Jim knelt down and cupped his hands to drink. He noticed an inviting sand bar a few yards upstream and headed for it.

Easing his backpack to the ground, he undressed and slipped into the cold water. It had the effect of numbing his scratches and insect bites, giving him a little relief. He rolled over on his back and floated slowly into an eddy. There was a wild mango tree on the other shore. He pulled two ripe mangoes down and ate them, savoring each sweet bite. The training films he had seen at camp came back to him as well as the words of the trainer:

"To some the jungle is a terror, full of evil and threat, ready to kill instantly anyone who happens to venture in." Nina had said at the banquet, quoting her father, "To others, who are wise and know its ways, the jungle is a veritable paradise. It is full of food and medicine and materials for shelter and all kinds of tools. Learn of these, and you could live in the jungle forever and never want for anything."

Jim stayed in the river for a long time. The mangoes were excellent for breakfast so he had one more for dessert. As he sat in the shallow water near the sand bar, the water flowed across his chest as just his head stuck out of the water. He thought of a picture in National Geographic he had seen as a boy. There was some kind of northern monkey neck deep in frigid water. His fur was spiked with ice and his red face was contorted in a fierce menacing grimace, intended to frighten the photographer.

Jim laughed, remembering the picture in his mind and then began to try to mimic the monkey faces. When he realized what he was doing, he laughed out loud and instantly felt the cut on his ribs. He put his hand to his side.

How, he wondered, could he be wailing and suicidal one moment and then laughing the next?

The Third Treasure

Perhaps dementia was setting in. Maybe he was cracking up under the strain. If he was going insane, he sure didn't feel like it. In fact, he felt in control! There was something fundamentally different about Jim, but he couldn't put his finger on it.

The morning sun was warming up, and Jim lay on the sand until he was dry. He snoozed a little, while watching for the vulture. The sand bar wound around the bend of the river and backed up against some large trees. Jim walked to the trees and hung the clothes he had rinsed in the river out to dry.

He explored the contents of his backpack. Finding some medicine, he treated the bigger cuts and scrapes on his body. He noted a couple of packs of crackers and granola bars. "The Three Treasures" fell out onto the sand, face down. Jim picked up the book and saw there was writing inside the cover.

"To Jim, with best regards. May you come to understand that the most important treasures are the ones that have nothing at all to do with our external circumstances. Your companion and friend, Weinberg."

"He sneaked in there and wrote this," said Jim, tears welling in his eyes.

He thumbed through the pages thoughtfully. The power of Weinberg's selfless sacrifice was impossible to rationalize in worldly terms. He could have saved himself. Instead he chose, voluntarily, to give his life for his friend.

He paused at the "Treasure of the Heart" and silently read the words again. They seemed to come to life in his hands as it became clear what was meant by the power of loving and sacrificially giving to others. Jim recalled the words of Weinberg as he thought about the monks at the monastery.

"What incredibly valuable lives," he had said.

That was the exact legacy he would assign to Weinberg. Jim now realized his sadness was for himself, not for Weinberg. Jim was alone and missed his friend, but he knew with a wonderful certainty that the older man was keeping the appointment he said he had with his wife. Knowing this gave him an overpowering sense of well being.

Reaching the end of the "Treasure of The Heart" he came to the third treasure. Turning the page he saw the title, "The Treasure of the Spirit." Jim had never read this last part of the book. He was too turned off by religion so he had not wanted to hear about this "spirit-stuff."

With his wet clothes drying and the mood created by finding Weinberg's autograph, Jim sat in the sand next to the river and read on.

The Treasure of The Spirit

And you will seek Me and find Me, when you search for Me with your heart. — Jeremiah 29:13.

If you have begun to gather treasures of the heart, you have started to realize the incredible power in the discipline of self-denial and seeking the welfare of others. Of those who embark on this journey, many

travelers stop at the Treasure of the Heart. Some have become great humanitarians, making valuable contributions to society. Others have simply lived this principle out in their corners of the world, becoming pillars of communities or just very well-liked friends.

If you should stop and not pursue this last treasure, you will be making the most tragic of errors! There will come a point in your life when you will find solace nowhere in the first two. You will ache inside in a way only those who have felt this pain can know.

We have discovered that even after fame, friends, money, and all manner of accomplishment, one must stand before the mirror and answer two questions. One, how do I find absolution in this life for the things I have done for which I am ashamed. Two, what is to become of me at my death. There is one answer to both questions.

The answer lies in the truth. Of late, truth has been diluted by those that say that all truth is relative. That is absurd. If I were to take your watch and claim that "my truth" says you are to release it to me, in fact, my truth tells me you will be better off for learning this particular giving lesson, you would cry "foul!"

You would see instantly that there is a larger body of truth that governs our world. We all know it is wrong to steal, but how? The laws against stealing, though man made, are inspired by a higher law that we all know. Witness the fact that even when the law does not catch us doing wrong we feel guilty... to whom?

Guilty to the truth. Wrong in the everpresence of right. Where do we go to get square with the first question and to find the answer to the second? We believe you must go to ancient scripture. When Pontius Pilate stood and asked the carpenter from Nazareth, "What is truth?" he was unknowingly making a statement to the world about the silent prisoner and the pride of man. Truth was standing in front of him, but he refused to see.

The carpenter told his followers he was sent from God. He said " I am the way, the truth, and the life, no man cometh to the Father but by me." If you or I were to make this claim, we would have some serious challenges on our hands. A decision must be made. There are three options: one, he was insane and deluded, which hardly squares with the incredible clarity of his life and words; two, he was a liar who knew he was lying and was willing to die for this absurd fantasy; or, three, he really was who he claimed to be.

Upon examination of his life and words, the first two options seem unlikely. If the third is true, then it is imperative that he be sought. In The Treasure of the Heart we are given the road that leads to joy. In The Treasure of the Spirit we are called by the Master to walk this road and respond to his simple words, "Follow me."

Beware the false roads and false leaders! They are persuasive and attractive because they appeal to human pride and reason. There is but one truth and one way that leads to life! It sounds huge and im-

possible, to travel with this power. Pilate's drama reveals to us that truth is not a concept; Truth is a person. The miracle is that the moment you begin to seek him with all your Heart, the finding is already thus assured!

Jim replaced the small book in his pack and sat very, very still. He looked across the river at a tree that had been invaded by beautiful yellow and crimson birds. They were singing a sweet and primitive song and hopping from branch to branch. The awesomeness of nature seem to speak to Jim and assure him that the song was for him alone. He smiled and gathered his clothes from the tree and dressed.

Buoyed by the morning respite, Jim decided to follow the river. He looked upstream and downstream. Logic said the river would empty into the sea somewhere, so Jim chose downstream perhaps because it looked like the upstream path might take him back toward the panther.

He hiked the route for the rest of the day, collecting fruits and other edibles on the way. His jungle training began to come back to him in this clearer frame of mind and his confidence returned with each small victory. Confidence aside, however, as darkness drew down on him, he was painfully aware that he was still completely lost.

Like a traveler who starts to evaluate the motels and restaurants he passes, he began looking out for a good place to camp for the night. Worry returned and nagged him. What if the river drew dangerous beasts, nocturnal hunters, toward him if he camped next to the stream? He would need to build a fire. Would the fire draw the poachers? Maybe it would draw a rescue? He decided to take the risk.

Finding a safe looking place where he could get his back to a stone outcropping, Jim lowered his pack to mark the spot and began to gather wood in the area. He spied a dead tree leaning across the bend in the river ahead and headed there. As he reached the tree, he heard a distant crashing sound. He cautiously moved down the river to the ever-increasing volume of the noise. The river had widened and deepened as he had followed it that day, but now it was moving much faster. Then he found the source of the sound.

The jungle opened up into a huge canyon, and the water fell right over the edge of the cliff. A waterfall! Jim smiled, thinking of all the cartoons where the unwitting character accidentally goes over the edge. He stepped out of the water sheepishly as if some force might sweep him over the top, and moved up along the bank to the overlook. What a magnificent view!

The waterfall was very high and hard to look at from the top. He gazed across the canyon and thought how much it looked like the place where he and Weinberg had sat and talked. Then he spied the stone bench across the gorge and the road that led back to the monastery.

Wait a minute. It was the exact, same valley! Only now he was on the opposite side! He let out a yell and waved his hat over his head. He knew where he was! The joy of discovery mixed with the sadness he felt for losing his companion rushed together as he looked out on the special place.

Recalling the jeep they had seen from the stone benches, he looked down the ridge to his right and, sure enough, way down there was the little dirt road where he had seen the Jeep! He recalled seeing a walking path along this side of the valley that would lead down to the road. He could be on the road in about two hours!

Looking back up the river where he had left his pack, he knew it would be dark before he could descend the steep path. It would be extremely dangerous to try to navigate the trail at night. He would not risk disaster this close to victory. He would camp here at this lovely spot and make it down at sunrise. Perhaps someone would see his fire and send rescue in the morning.

Jim found lots of wood nearby and soon had a fine fire. He managed to boil some water in a small cup and added the leaves he had found to make an aromatic Wild African Tea. Munching on his harvest of the day, he waited for the tea to cool. He leaned back on the log near the fire and looked out at the beautiful valley. What had Weinberg said about it?

Oh, yes, he had said there were some places on earth where you could see the hand of God more clearly than others. Well, this was definitely one of them. There was more than the natural beauty of the place. There was the incredible value of the brief time he had spent here with dear Weinberg. There was the hope he felt for finding the road that would lead him to safety. But, there was more.

Jim reached for the still hot tea and took a sip. "Wow, that's hot!" he shouted to no one. But the feeling was as good as the pungent taste so he smacked his lips and went right back for another. Setting the cup on the rock next to him like a little coffee table, he tried to gather in his feelings.

He thought of something Weinberg had said at breakfast the second day of the safari. He had written it in his journal although it didn't seem to mean much then.

"Sometimes the most significant moments of our lives go right by unnoticed," he had said, "because we are too busy heading somewhere totally trivial. Usually the most valuable moments in life are only seen in hindsight. They are sweet enough when we look back on them, but how much richer life is when we are actually there, in the moment. We must learn to taste, feel, and sense them as they happen. This way we heighten the experience, extend the moment and capture it in a richer, deeper way, that will last forever."

Jim closed the journal and remembered Weinberg's explanation.

"The words of a child," he had said, "the touch of a loved one, the unexpected opportunity and privilege to view the intensely vivid reality of life displayed by nature and chance. Feel your feet on the floor, your hand on the table, and the wind as it touches your

The Third Treasure

face. Hear the sounds, and smell the smells. You can magnify the richness of the life you are already experiencing if you will commit, whenever you think of it, to consciously be wherever you are."

Jim let his eyes shift their focus and tried to amplify all his senses. A feeling of peace and contentment washed over him and bathed him in its power. He opened his eyes and knew what it was that he was feeling. The power of this place was only partially the answer. Jim realized that he was actually feeling good about himself.

He was somehow different now that he had faced ultimate fear and survived. He felt the muscles in his arms and legs and knew he had been given the gift of a healthy body. He thought of all he had learned and would continue to learn with his new commitment to read books and listen to tapes when he returned home. His mind would become the engine that would transform his life.

His heart had melted at the story Weinberg had told about his marriage. He was already planning how to mend fences with Tracey and the kids. He had been the beneficiary of the greatest gift at the dearest price when Weinberg had saved his life. Never again would he be the same. He would do his best to become a giving, caring person and try to be worthy of the sacrifice this great man had made for him.

But the real difference was somewhere deep inside Jim's soul. "If anyone had told me I would be sitting alone, cut, scraped, and out of supplies at nightfall, lost in the jungle of Africa and yet happy, I would have told them they were crazy," he thought. But it was true. He was strangely happy and content.

Reaching into his pack for the medicinal ointment, his hand discovered Weinberg's Bible. He pulled it out and looked at the cover. It was worn and soft from many hours of use. Benjamin had kidded him about its ragged condition back at the lodge and offered to buy him a new one.

"A Bible that is falling apart usually belongs to someone who isn't!" Weinberg had replied with his wink and thumbs up and smile.

It occurred to him that he was holding a most precious keepsake that had become his to watch over now. Opening it carefully, reverently, he saw that there were lots of handwritten notes in the margins and hi-lighted verses in various markers and ink colors. It never occurred to him that anyone would write in a Bible. There were dates and names of speakers and little drawings and arrows indicating devotion and careful study.

The thin, delicate, pages crackled and turned easily to his careful touch. The book seemed so ancient and intense here beside the waterfall in the vast wilderness.

Jim turned to the table of contents and found the Gospel According to John. Benjamin had said that was a good place to start so he turned there and read the first three tiny chapters. He was instantly challenged by the words, "He came unto His own, and they knew Him not."

How strange, that the people who had expected

The Third Treasure

their Messiah for years, rejected him when he actually came. Jim thought about how that was kind of true in his own life. How many times had the simple message of salvation come to him while he ignored and scoffed at it?

Suddenly he felt like thanking God, but he didn't know how. He thought about his father and mother. They had taken him to church off and on, but it didn't seem to mean much to them. They never talked about spiritual things, and Jim had never seen them pray anywhere outside of church. Jim too hadn't prayed since grade school and then only under the watchful eye of a hopeful Sunday School teacher.

He felt silly, but began with, "Now I lay me down to sleep..."and then stopped.

"If you seek me with all your heart, you will find me," the third treasure had promised. If the heart meant the selfless giving to others that was totally outside of yourself, then seeking with the heart must mean you stop focusing on you, and search for God outside of yourself, on His terms.

Jim began again. This time he prayed a very humble prayer of thanks for all the things he had been given in his life. The more he listed, the more powerful and heartfelt were his words. He began to realize just how fortunate he was. He asked to be able to return home to his family and to make amends there. He asked for strength to follow the ideas in "The Three Treasures."

Then he became silent. With his eyes closed he said, "These guys say, that you said, if I will look for you with all of my heart, I will find you. Well, I am going to find out if that is true because I am going to try it. The first thing I'm going to do when I get back is to read this Bible they say you wrote and look that up, and see if it's there. Then, if it is, I'm going to read the whole thing. The rest is up to you. Thanks again. Amen."

When he opened his eyes, he had that instant, funny feeling you get when you enter a movie theater in the daylight and find it dark when you come out. Though he had only prayed a short time, the sun had dipped below the trees behind him. In the cooler air, crickets began making sounds like a rusty hinge on an old screen door. The jungle prepared for another night.

Pulling the small tin cup to his lips, he cautiously sampled the tea. It was just right. The sun was burning a laser show on the rock face below the stone bench across the canyon. The whole scene was breathtaking. No photograph in the world could capture its exhilarating color and texture. Every time he looked at a different area, it seemed to change with the sinking sun and made for an almost liquid clarity.

The sky melted from pink to orange, to red, and then into darkness. The sun was replaced by a quarter moon that lit the valley in an eerie, luminescent stillness. When his daughter, Claire, was little, he remembered they had been driving home, just the two of them. She was probably five or six. She had looked up and seen this shape of moon and proudly announced,

"Look, Daddy! A nickel moon!"

The Third Treasure

How he had treasured that innocence and joy. He had patiently explained what a quarter moon was. She had laughed with him, and the nickel moon became their private little joke. They had even made up a little song about it. He sang it softly.

> *I can almost see,*
> *A place where we can go together,*
> *You and Mom and me.*
> *Take short pants—you'll love the weather*
> *Bears that care, and ponies fly,*
> *We can go right now.*
>
> *Daddy, why do people work?*
> *Always seem in such a hurry,*
> *Don't they play no more?*
> *Tired faces lined in worry—*
> *Sit down here with me,*
> *Teddy's having tea*
> *Under the nickel moon,*
> *Live on soda pop and candy,*
> *Under the nickel moon,*
> *Right next door to Ann and Andy*
> *Bears that care, and ponies fly,*
> *We can go right now.*
>
> *Daddy, why you look so sad?*
> *Don't you think that we can go there?*
> *Growing up's not bad*
> *A part of us should always stay where,*
> *We can always be,*
> *Young and wild and free!*
> *Under the nickel moon,*
> *Live on soda pop and candy,*
> *Under the nickel moon,*
> *Right next door to Ann and Andy*
> *Bears that care, and ponies fly,*
> *We can go right now.*

His voice broke at the last line. His throat would not let him go on singing. He bowed his head and sat quietly for a long time, then he started to write in his journal. A flood of thoughts and impressions came too quickly for his pen. He tried to recall all Weinberg's words and wrote down what he could.

Before he stopped to sleep, he wrote a long love-letter to Tracey. Feeling like a World War I doughboy writing from a foxhole in Europe, he romantically said all the things he wished he had told her when he had the chance. He described her beauty, their special names for one another, and how he treasured the secret moments only the two of them could ever know.

He savored the preciousness of the hard times when they were young, trying to work and raise the babies. He boldly poured out his heart to his wife in case the journal was found, and he had not made it out alive. His heart was filled with such powerful love and emotion. He could not help but cry again.

This time tears of joy and hope and love replaced the bitter sorrow he had tasted only this morning. He wiped his eyes with the soft handkerchief from his pocket, sat back and took a deep breath. He replaced the journal in his pack and made it his pillow. Fiddling with the fire for a bit, he drank the last of the tea and never knew it when sleep came.

Dangerous Rescue

Jim wasted no time in putting out the smoldering fire and starting down the trail to the road. The sun, now rising on the opposite side of the valley, lit and warmed the face of the wall he was climbing. "I wish I had some sunglasses," he thought, then another thought replaced it that made him smile. "But, I am sure glad I have eyes!" His new attitude was energizing. He looked for ways to replace the negative thoughts he normally had with new, powerful, positive ones.

Sure enough, the path led down to the road. He could glimpse the road every time the path wound to the outside of the ledge as he carefully descended. It was a trail, but it was pretty rough going. He would have been crazy to try to take this path in the dark last night. He calculated that he would be down to the road in about a half hour. Then it would be only a matter of time until he either came to the half-way station or a friendly jeep came along. He felt strong and confident that the end was near.

Suddenly, the air was pierced by a shriek. Where had he heard the sound before? It sounded like the cry made by Karin back at the camp when the tent fell in on her. Loud and begging, it was the wail of a woman screaming for her life. The sound echoed across the canyon. Jim stopped and tried to pinpoint its origin.

The Safari Adventure Company

Gunshots rang out, then a crazy whoop, followed by a wicked laughter. There in the valley, on the other side of the river, were two people running. One of them was Karin!

She was being chased by one of the poachers. It was not the same one he had shot at before falling down the cliff. The long haired, filthy bandit was short and stout and gaining fast on the ragged girl. Her clothes were tattered and torn. The poacher stopped briefly and fired his gun around her and laughed sadistically. It was obvious as she stumbled and fell that she was exhausted and terrorized. The torture continued.

She was trying to run up the path on the side of the valley where Jim and Weinberg had sat so idyllically just a few days and a thousand years ago. She was only a few meters from the top, but the path there was steep and she slipped and slid down right into the hands of the poacher.

Jim crouched, frozen in the bushes, too far away to do anything else. He watched the man brutally punch her face and knock her unconscious. He then pulled a piece of cord from his pack and tied first her hands then ankles together tightly. That was when Jim saw the other two men standing right where he and Weinberg had sat by the flowers. What absolute horror she must have been in as she tried to escape the trap.

The larger man picked her up and slung her over his shoulder easily. The trio disappeared back up the path toward the monastery.

A thousand excuses went through Jim's mind. How could he expect to do anything about Karin? He was weak and exhausted himself. His hand traced the wound from the panther's claws. He could save himself and no one would ever know! He looked longingly down the jeep road to freedom. No one would know. "No one but me," he thought to himself.

Then a new thought came to his mind—a thought of pure courage. He could not go on to safety knowing the girl was in the hands of these savage men. He would do the right thing. He would give everything he had to save her! The minute he made the decision the knots in his stomach tightened and threatened to make him ill, but he fought his own fear with confident action.

He descended the rest of the path quickly and paddled hard across the rapidly moving river with the help of a log to keep his pack dry and reached the top of the cliff in an hour. Stopping briefly to catch his breath at the stone bench, he surveyed the waterfall one more time. He had been certain he would never see the waterfall again, and the power of the place swept over him once more. He instantly flashed on the vision of Weinberg sitting next to him and saying, "There are some places where you can see the hand of God," he had said, "this is mine."

Jim realized that another place you could see God's hand at work was in the life of a person who had voluntarily chosen to give themselves to someone else, regardless of the cost. Weinberg had painted this beautiful picture with his rescue of Jim from the panther. Then he knew Weinberg was only painting one more time the original work of Jesus. He would not waste the gift!

"I know I was not worth the price Weinberg paid," thought Jim, "but, he didn't save me because of who I was, but because of the great treasure of sacrificial giving to the one in need. He didn't even think twice. The decision was made long ago."

The thought was like a lightning bolt of strength. He leapt up from the stone bench and committed himself down the path toward the monastery. He would not turn back!

The sun was high when he peered over the last hill and saw the monastery. The air was hot and sticky. His shirt clung to his skin drenched with perspiration. Jim had no plan. He was just going to show up and do what he could. There was no sign of the poachers or Karin, so he made his way into the bushes where he and Weinberg had spent that awful night. He couldn't help but look at the ashes of the bonfire, but, thankfully, there was nothing left of the body to see.

He pulled the pistol out and released the safety. Jim had never even owned a gun. He rarely hunted with friends, but the grip felt good in his hand. He would shoot the poachers, if he had to! That's all there was to it. There might be only the three of them left since they had killed one of their own and he might have shot the other. Jim realized he was hoping that he had killed the man in the forest. He was operating completely out of character now.

Rounding the corner of the monastery, he saw the secret passage where he and Weinberg had escaped. He started to squeeze in when a jolt of intense fear iced him where he stood.

Dear God, he thought, what if they catch me and kill me?

But, what if this were Tracey, or Claire?

What if they were in great danger and needed a rescuer. Wouldn't I pray that a stranger would take action?

Of course!

But, why me?

Oh, God! Why me?

Right in the middle of his old nature screaming out in fear and selfishness, Jim saw the awful reality of the situation, and grasped it. Just then a divine guidance, beyond his own understanding or experience, filled him with the courage and strength, not to run, but to face his terror and act.

He understood clearly that in the entire world of people, he was the one and only person on the planet who could do anything to help this poor, doomed girl. The "old Jim", weak and afraid, died right there on the spot. He prayed for strength and safety, swallowed hard, and slipped into the small opening in the side of the stone monastery and plunged into the blackness of the monk's cell.

The damp coolness of the place jumped on his sweaty shirt and skin. He waited for his eyes to adjust to the darkness, then flipped on Weinberg's flashlight and crept cautiously down the hallway like a cat burglar. Gun drawn and pointed he shoved his canvas pack back up on his shoulder and began to look into each room.

No sight or sound of either Karin or the poachers. He looked over the last room and turned his head toward the chapel. The colored stones were bathing the chapel in a rainbow of fragile color. The gun boxes had been opened, and several of the rifles had been scattered across the pews in the front. Most of the tusks were gone. The poachers had been very busy.

Turning back down the hall, Jim stopped and strained to hear anything at all.

Silence.

There was still one room past the passageway he had not checked. He slipped softly down the hall and shined the light into the small cell. The words, "I can do all things through Christ, who strengthens me," were right in the center of his light. Jim mouthed the words silently as he read them.

Forcing his eyes to look into the dim shadows, he saw Karin huddled against the wall in a fetal position, silent and still.

"Please, please, don't let her be dead," he thought.

He moved quickly to her side and touched her face. It was streaked with blood, dirt, and tears—whether from the poachers or her days in the jungle, he could not tell. He marveled at her courage. He was a 6' 2" man; he had almost died. She was only a small, young girl. How in the world had she survived?

Her bound hands shot up to her face as she opened her eyes, seeing only the flashlight.

She flinched and whimpered, "Please don't hurt me anymore," covering her face.

"Karin," he whispered, "it's me, Jim." He pulled the flashlight out of her face and pointed it up, bathing the room in a soft yellow dimness.

"Oh, God!" she said half choking, "I can't believe it. How in the world did you get here?"

Her feisty spirit had been practically extinguished as her hope had faded. After being lost for days in the jungle and captured by the poachers, she had started to believe she was going to die at the end of unthinkable captivity.

Lifting his finger to his lips, he gave her the sign for silence.

"Where are the poachers?" he whispered quickly, cutting the rope from her hands with his pocketknife.

"I heard them talking after they threw me in here. Two of them were going to the village to get whiskey. I don't know where the other one is," she said, frantically untangling the ropes and reaching for the cord around her ankles.

"Are there three or four?" he asked hopefully.

"Just three."

"Okay, let's get out of here. There's a secret passageway to the outside. We just have to go back into the hall and into the next room. Follow me."

With that, Jim helped her to her feet. She was bruised badly, but the determination that made her so tough became her friend. Jim took her arm and led her to the door.

"Okay, let's go," said Jim. It looked like a perfect escape from the monastery when he heard the shout.

"Aiyee-ahhhh!" came the warlike scream from the guarding poacher. Jim shined the flashlight toward the sound. He came from the direction of the front courtyard and was heading straight for them down the narrow passageway. The flashlight reflected back a laser glint off the biggest machete Jim had ever seen in his life.

Jim pushed Karin behind him toward the way to safety and turned to face the rushing attacker. She ran. With no way of knowing, she shot past the room with the escape door, and headed toward the chapel at the end of the hallway. They were trapped!

Jim spun around and pulled his pistol to fire, but the machete caught his arm with a glancing blow off the wall and knocked the gun from his hand. As it clattered on the stone floor, blood spurted from the gash. Jim cried out and put his other hand on the wound as an instant reaction.

The Safari Adventure Company

The poacher laughed. Jim knew instantly from the sound that this was the sadistic torturer who had fired at Karin as he chased her—the one who had coldly punched the helpless girl! He looked at the stubble-bearded face and the yellow stained teeth and realized that all his misfortune, the death of Weinberg, Karin and his burning arm, were all the fault of the evil man in front of him.

Instead of running, Jim doubled his fist and smashed old yellow teeth right in the mouth. Blood drained out of the startled poacher's mouth. Fire shot up Jim's arm from the blow as his fist was cut on the foul teeth. Before the attacker could recover from the punch, Jim kicked him solidly in the groin.

Remarkably, the poacher, shouting in hatred, caught Jim's leg and threw him quickly on his back. Jim scrambled to feel for the pistol, but it was gone. He rolled on his side just as the shrill clang of the machete blow sent sparks from the stone floor in the dark hallway by his head.

He half crawled, half ran, furiously toward the chapel. The shrieking poacher was right on his heels. Out of the corner of his eye, he saw Karin pressed flat against the wall just inside the doorway. As the bandit reached the entrance, she swung the rifle by the barrel like a baseball bat with all her might and smashed the stock of the heavy gun into the poacher's face. The impact of the strike combined with his running momentum knocked the poacher off his feet and flat on his back.

Jim watched in shock as she took her redemption. In one motion she spun the gun around in her hand and fired every round into the lurching body until both the gun and the devilish fiend were silent. Jim thought of the panther and understood. In one horrible moment, she destroyed the destroyer. Jim never knew what happened to her at the hands of the men, and he never asked.

There in the stained glass light of the chapel Karin stood, eyes wide, chest heaving as she panted heavily. Staring down at her dead tormentor, she dropped the hot, smoking gun and began to weep. She drew her clinched fists to her temples and moaned in anguish. It was the most heartbreaking sound Jim had ever heard.

He ran to her side and held her as the biting sulphur smell of gunpowder permeated the room. Finally, she calmed down enough to follow him out to the passage to freedom.

Knowing that the other two poachers had only been gone a short time, Jim led Karin back up the trail to the waterfall where they rested and tended to each other's wounds. Jim was badly cut from the machete, but she fixed a rough tourniquet that stopped the bleeding. He used the medicine he had in his bag to take the sting out of her many cuts. She was not as seriously hurt as he thought at first. She was, however, very dehydrated and hadn't eaten much in the days since the attack.

She told Jim how the poachers had come upon them late that morning. They wore masks and intended to rob the safari. When the little man with the wicked laugh grabbed her at the campsite and started to drag her away, Rosa had stepped in and slapped him. A fight broke out. Then gunshots. Everyone ran into the jungle in chaos. She never saw any of the group again. She had wandered in circles and was just about to give up when she was spotted by the poachers.

The Safari Adventure Company

"You saved my life, Jim. I am so very, very thankful for you. God bless you. I will never forget what you did for me. You could have left me behind and not risked your life, but you did. Thank you, Jim, thank you, from the bottom of my heart."

As she hugged his neck, Jim knew in a new way what "The Treasure of the Heart" was all about. He was receiving something wonderful that only came from giving. The power of the moment would last forever!

Jim reminded her that she had saved his life, too! Her quick thinking in the chapel saved them both. He was very grateful. He told her the story of what happened to Weinberg as they headed back to the road down the path that had started it all.

She wondered aloud about Rosa. They were just beginning to build a friendship. Was she alive? What about the others?

They emerged from the jungle at the original campsite. Except for the burned out jeep it was picked clean. The body of the guide was gone.

Jim told Karin how he had taken up some things from here as he doubled back. They agreed, though, that the poachers had probably returned and cleaned the site of all the supplies and equipment.

Then they saw the sign.

"Please stay near the road. We are searching for you," it announced. At the bottom of the stick that held it was a backpack filled with food, medicine and supplies. They joyfully gathered up the wonderful care package, as they called it, ate a little and decided to get as far from the campsite as they could.

Shadows crossed the road and they began to wearily search for a place to camp for the night. The tired adventurers were headed in the direction of the lake again. This time they descended alone. No poachers with rifles greeted them as they walked.

The going was easy here on the jeep road, but Jim stayed alert. He listened for the sound of danger. They agreed that if they heard a vehicle they would hide in the bushes and look to see if it were carrying poachers or not. He would rather walk all the way if necessary than take a chance of falling prey to them again. They would surely be out to kill after what they must have found by now at the monastery.

Suddenly, they heard the unmistakable sound of a Land Rover. Leaping into the jungle, they realized that they had just turned a corner and would not be able to identify the occupants until just as the jeep was passing. If the driver was friendly, they would then have to jump out and try to flag them down in a split second, just as they passed. They crouched hopefully, ready to spring. Jim prayed silently for a friendly face.

Drawing closer, the whine of the engine lowered and then started rising again as the driver down shifted to make the hill. Just as the jeep came into sight, Jim saw two of the men he recognized from the Safari Adventure Company looking straight ahead.

Jim sprang out of the bush just as they passed and called out loudly, nearly hitting the back of the jeep with his hand. The men never saw him as he stood in the road and danced and waved his hands, screaming at the top of his lungs.

"Don't leave us!" they cried, "Hey! Hey! Help! Help! Help!"

The blaring horn behind them made them both jump and spin around suddenly in shock.

A second jeep!

It darted away and barely missed hitting Jim at

full speed. He leaped and fell away on the side of the road and lay there with his heart pounding. All that he had been through to die in a car wreck a thousand miles from a traffic light!

"I was nearly killed, again!" he thought as he tried to stand.

"Jim! My God, Jim! Is that you?" called a familiar voice. The jeep, which had stopped, was now backing up toward him. "Oh, thank God, it is!"

Jim rolled over and sat up on his elbow just as Benjamin and Stephen bailed out of each side of the jeep and ran to his side.

"How in the world did you come to be here?" cried Benjamin. "We have been lookin' all over for you!"

"It's a long story, Benjamin. Man, is it good to see your face, and jeep!" said Jim as the men helped him to his feet gingerly.

The others from the first jeep were attending to Karin, who had no complaints, this time, about anything.

"Where is Weinberg?" Benjamin asked cautiously as he saw the blood and cuts all across Jim's battered body.

"He is dead, Benjamin," said Jim sadly. "He was killed by a panther. He took my place. He saved my life." Now that he was safe, the words stuck in his throat as the magnitude of the whole experience began to dawn on him.

"Come on, man, let's get you back to camp." He placed his arm around Jim's waist and guided him back to the Rover. Benjamin and Stephen loaded Jim carefully into the back seat and arranged their supplies so he could lie back comfortably.

Stephen filled in the rest of the story. He told Jim

how the poachers had come upon them and held them up at gun point. They wore masks and would have gotten everything with no resistance from the group until one of them began to grab Karin. Rosa slapped him and was shoved to the ground. Ishido, the younger Japanese man had kicked the tormentor in the face and everything broke loose into confusion. The group scattered in fear and ran into the jungle in different directions, while Ishido and Gabriel fought with the poachers.

Gabriel was shot and killed and Ishido was wounded and left for dead. The poachers stole what they could. They took two of the jeeps—one wouldn't start and they figured it was broken down. They set the other one on fire.

It was then that Jim saw the large bandage on Stephen's shoulder under his oversized shirt. He did not have to ask what had happened to him. Benjamin explained how Stephen, seriously wounded, had tried valiantly to gather the scattered band and bring them back to safety.

Jim realized he and Weinberg had arrived after the group had returned to camp. It was total coincidence that they had not run into each other before the storm.

Jim thought about the intensity of the storm that night as Stephen told how he rounded up everyone but Karin. They they drove the roads looking for signs of their companions until finally they gave up and left the area to get Ishido to a doctor.

Stephen had volunteered to return to the area to get his friend's body and to search for the three lost ones. He was very grateful to find Jim and Karin. Somehow it seemed to lighten the load of responsibility he felt as the emergency leader of the group.

The Safari Adventure Company

The Safari Company put up such an uproar that the government authorities were forced to do something and were tracking down the poachers even now. Jim told the men about the monastery hide-out.

"Now it is over," said Stephen as he guided the jeep along the dusty road. "Now that everyone has been found, things can get back to normal around here."

"Back to normal?" thought Jim. Things would never be back to normal again in his life. The steady drone of the engine, excitement and fatigue, took their toll on Jim. He slumped back on the blankets and drifted into sleep as the driver guided the jeep down the road toward the station.

OVER AND OUT!

"Hey, wait a minute! Stop! I need to talk to that guy!" Despite the noise of the rotors Jim heard the voice behind him as he was stepping up onto the deck of the helicopter. He turned to see Andy running toward the aircraft, his huge smile unmistakable from across the landing zone. Benjamin trailed him by a few steps.

"Hey, lightweight, you taking the sissy way home?" he kidded loudly. "I can't believe you are going to wimp out on me!"

"Yeah, Andy, I am going to leave Africa to the real hosses like you!" He smiled back warmly as Andy and he pumped each other's hands. "They said you had come back here and joined the search party for me. Thanks so much! Thank you both."

"Have you talked to your wife yet?" said Andy.

"Not yet. We played radio tag though," Jim said referring to the wireless set at the half-way station. They told me she was frantic when she heard I was lost.

"Some guys will do anything to get attention," kidded Andy, winking.

"Jim, I am afraid we will have to charge you double. You were not supposed to have such an intense safari," Benjamin joked.

"Seriously, my friend, I am so sorry you had to go through what you have," Benjamin said patting Jim's

The Safari Adventure Company

good arm briskly.

"Thanks, Benjamin. I'm okay. I am just trying to process everything. Thank you for taking the time for me back at the lake. Your words meant a lot. There's a bigger reason why I experienced what I did."

"I like you, Jim. You have come a long way. Give me a call in a couple of weeks, after you are up and around. I think I have an idea for a job you may be very interested in." Benjamin stepped along the landing gear to talk to Karin who was already in the passenger seat next to the pilot.

"Jim, I found what I was looking for all these years," said Andy seriously. "Except it wasn't in Africa at all, buddy, it was right here, all along." Andy pointed to the center of his chest.

"I know what you mean. I found it, too," said Jim. Still shaking hands, both men reached their free arm around the other and hugged tightly for an extra moment.

Stepping up on the deck of the helicopter, Jim turned around and saw the light in the eyes of his friend. They each knew that they had both indeed found the truth that had been missing all their lives. Andy and Benjamin hugged Karin. They stepped back and saluted her. She smiled broadly and waved back.

"So long Andy," shouted Jim over the helicopter engines as they began to rev up. "I guess the adventure is over."

"No way, Jim!" shouted Andy over the clatter. "Don't you understand? The greatest adventure is the rest of your life!"

The helicopter lifted up slowly and banked to the East toward Lilongwe and the Kamuzu Airport. Jim watched as Andy waved until he disappeared under the sweeping forest. As he looked down on the place where he had spent the last few terrifying days, he took a moment to reflect on the intense power of the human desire to live.

The beautiful waterfall appeared below as Jim shook his head in disbelief. Who would believe his amazing tale? Though he was down there only a few short hours ago, already it started to seem surreal and dreamlike.

He knew, however, that he was different. Right down the center of his being he would never, ever, be the same again.

As he settled back, his thoughts turned to Tracey and the kids. He knew what his destiny held. He would turn his mind to truth and wisdom. He would learn to be the best husband, father, and person, he could be. He had faith that the simple act of giving, repeated over time, would open his life like a fountain of meaning and power. It would not be easy to repair years of neglect. But, he would stay the course.

Finally he knew that he was already standing in the doorway of spiritual truth. He put his hand in his jacket and pulled out Weinberg's tattered Bible. Of all the insane events of the last two weeks, the fact that he now held this precious book from that incredible man, was unexplainable by any other means, but one.

There was a force far greater than anything Jim had ever known, that was drawing him into total clarity and reality. In the words of the Third Treasure,

"The miracle is that the moment one begins to seek with all their heart, the finding is already thus assured!

Jim tucked the Bible back into his jacket and closed his eyes. The road ahead was going to be tough; he had no illusions. Now, though, he knew he would win!

He pulled his wide brimmed safari hat, his dusty and scratched companion that had witnessed it all, down tightly on his head against the wind and softly hummed the nickel moon.

As the helicopter banked and crossed the Lake of Stars, Andy's final words came back to Jim.

> "THE GREATEST ADVENTURE IS
> THE REST OF YOUR LIFE!"

Yes, there is a second book...

For more information
contact Adventure Seminars

About the Author

Rick Butts

Once in a lifetime someone comes along that radically shifts our world view, forcing us to challenge the assumptions that have ceased to serve us. Electrifying author and speaker, Rick Butts, has been called one of the most original thinkers of the decade.

Audiences everywhere are talking about his unforgettable live presentations filled with laughter, emotion, and powerful ideas you can use immediately!

Successful entrepreneur, business owner, author, financial consultant, sales champion, pig farmer, lumberjack, and pastor, Rick's wide experiences all started as a "long hair rock and roll guitarist/singer!"

You can experience the power of the Safari by having Rick speak at your next event, or attend one of his exhilarating Rocky Mountain Retreats!

To join the Safari Adventure Co. (It's FREE!) and get discounts on books, tapes, and rocky mountain retreats, or get more information about Rick's programs at E-mail: rick@butts.com or http://www.butts.com or call 1-800-442-6214.

Rick Butts
Adventure Seminars

Did you ever get a great idea from a book or seminar... and never use it? Find out how to "IMPLEMENT" your big plans with the awesome power of: "THE I-FACTOR". On line info at http://www.butts.com (and a FREE: sneak peek at hot new book!)

To order more copies of:
The Safari Adventure Company
fax copies of this form with your credit card information to (409) 826-4030 or mail a check to: Adventure Seminars, Route 1, Box 188A, Waller, Texas 77484

Please send me _____ copies of
The Safari Aventure Company by Rick Butts

Cost per book	$14.95
Texas sales tax (8.25%)	$_____
Shipping ($3.00 ea. book)	$_____
Total cost	$_____

Send this order to:

Name _____

Company Name _____

Mailing Address _____

_____

City _____

State, Zip _____

Credit Card: VISA   M/C   AMEX

Card No. _____

Expiration date _____